Shameless

AF646136

Shameless

Salam Azad

Translated by
Poorvi Panwar

Srishti
Publishers & Distributors

Srishti Publishers & Distributors
64-A, Adhchini
Sri Aurobindo Marg
New Delhi 110 017
srishtipublishers@yahoo.com

First published in English by Srishti Publishers & Distributors in 2005
Copyright © original Bangla with Salam Azad
Copyright © English translation with Srishti Publishers & Distributors, 2005

ISBN 81-88575-48-8

Typeset in AGaramond 11pt. by Suresh Kumar Sharma at Srishti

Cover design: Vinayak Bhattacharya

Printed and bound in India

All rights reserved. No part of this publication may be reproduced, stored in a retrieval system, or transmitted, in any form or by any means, electronic, mechanical, photocopying, recording or otherwise, without the prior written permission of the Publishers.

Dedicated to Mirza Fahmida Azim Soheli

To whom I am overly grateful

For encouraging my literary efforts

Copyright: Mirza Fahmida Azim Soheli

One

Rahul Roy visited Dhaka as a journalist. The Delhi office of his newspaper had sent him to cover the National Assembly Elections in Bangladesh and he could stay on for a month, as per his visa. Everyday he would send his copy but never knew whether it was published or not. No Indian newspaper, including the one he worked for, was not allowed in Dhaka.But when he visited cyber cafes to send his copy, sometimes he visited the website of his newspaper. It made him glad to see that the news sent by him was given significant coverage. Of course he could not visit the website every day, sometimes he felt too exhausted to make the effort. Secondly, One had to pay three times more here in a cyber café as compared to Delhi or Kolkata. The differences between Bangladesh and India extended to many other fields as well and this touched Rahul deeply. Rahul's ancestors were from Barisal. In 1947 after the Partition of the country, his family migrated to Kolkata. Rahul was born and brought up there. He was staying in Delhi because of his job. In Kolkata one could buy small portions of curd or small quantities of fish or meat. In Dhaka it was not possible; one had to buy one kilogram of fish or meat and one whole container of curd. This astonished Rahul who considered it a waste, but of course he did not discuss it with anyone. He thought that people might not like him commenting on the practices in their country.

Rahul was not interested in the town of Bhola, though the land of his ancestors did attract him. He had been here for almost a month now – four more days to go. Was it possible to see everything and return to India within the stipulated period, Rahul asked himself. Before leaving Delhi he had spoken to his father in Kolkata, who had requested him more than once to visit Bhola and take a photograph of their ancestral house. He had promised his father that he would definitely visit Bhola. Now only four days were left. There was still some work pending in Dhaka. The Delhi office of his newspaper was asking him repeatedly to interview the newly elected Prime Minister. But even after a number of attempts this did not seem possible. He had not been able to give the Delhi office a substantial reason as to why he had not managed the interview. He himself was not satisfied with the copies he had sent. It seemed almost certain that he would not be able to manage the interview, but there was no harm trying once more. On that basis the Delhi office would give him permission to stay on in Dhaka for a few more days. But first the visa had to be extended. He rang up Bari to know how this could be facilitated. Of all the journalists he had met in Dhaka, he liked Bari considerably. Bari had promised that he would arrange for Rahul's visa to be extended the very next day. But when he told Bari that he wanted to go to Bhola,the latter bombarded him with questions.Bari was being sent to Bhola by his newspaper the day after tomorrow to assess the situation during the elections and send reports on it.

Rahul was quite reassured to learn that his trip to Bhola with Bari had been arranged. His visa was extended the next day but he had to answer a whole lot of questions. Bari had already warned him not to breathe a word of his trip to Bhola or for that matter, anywhere outside Dhaka to the officials in the Immigration Office. Rahul stuck to his earlier plea that he wanted to stay on for a few more days to see if he could get an appointment with the Prime Minister. In support of this he showed them a copy of his application requesting an interview with the Prime Minister. Along with the extension of his visa he emailed his Delhi office that he wanted permission to stay on in Dhaka for another fortnight. At the end of his email he asked for expenses for the period to be arranged.

Today Rahul had no work. He had already decided that he would not send any copy. The following evening he and Bari planned to leave for Bhola. It was an overnight journey by steamer, the next morning they would be in Bhola. He had never travelled such a long distance by steamer earlier, this would be the first time. Since he was free today, he intended to go around Dhaka. In the last month he had seen nothing in the city, nothing except the places where his work had taken him. Today he wanted to see it as a tourist, talk to people and get the feel of the place. That was what he did the whole day.

Finally when he returned to his hotel he was dead tired and very sleepy. But he could not go to sleep without a shower to wash off the dust and pollution. As soon as he went into the bathroom, the phone rang. It was his editor telling him that the permission had been granted. He would get the money the next day. But the editor insisted that he must interview the Prime Minister. Rahul said 'yes' and put down the phone though he knew very well that it was not possible to interview the Prime Minister at this juncture. He was rather upset and wondered why he had told his editor that he leave only after interviewing the Prime Minister.

Rahul received the money that the editor had referred to the previous night, in the afternoon. He got ready at exactly five o'clock. At a quarter past five Ahsanul Bari came to his hotel. The two of them took a rickshaw to Sadar Ghat from where they were to board a steamer to Bhola.

They came out of their cabins and stood on the deck as the steamer left Fhatulla and moved towards Bhola. Crossing the confluence of Burhi Ganga, Dhauleshwari and Shitalakshya rivers, the steamer moved on. Bari started the conversation.

"You are going there only to see your ancestral house?"

"Absolutely."

"You have no other work or assignment?"

"No."

"But why? Tell me."

"No, just like that. I was thinking about the important assignment that I have been given." Bari confided.

May I know what that assignment might be?" Rahul asked.

"Now I can tell you about it. In fact if you want, you can accompany me."

"Let me first know what the assignment is all about."

"We have got the information that all kinds of atrocities have been committed on Hindus right from the day following the election. We have to visit the spot, assess the situation and send in reports. I cannot say for sure how many days I might have to stop at Bhola."

Rahul responded very casually to Bari and said, "A friend in Dhaka has already told me all this. Not just once, but a number of times. But I did not show any interest."

"Why?" Bari wanted to know.

"If I write about it, maybe I will never get a visa to come back to Dhaka even if I want to."

Bari looked up and said, "Do you know about the extent of the atrocities committed? From the reports we have received, about forty lakh Hindus have been affected."

"What are you saying? The number of Hindus who voted is over seventy lakh."

"The number of Hindus who cast their votes is higher. Around one crore and twentyfive lakh. But due to a number of reasons, about four hundred and seventy five Hindus are leaving Bangladesh for good. These are the statistics in normal times. But after the first of October last, the situation is not normal."

"You mean to say that every year from your country..."

Rahul stopped in the middle of a sentence. He went to his cabin, took out his calculator and started calculating. Around one lakh seventy three thousand three hundred and seventy five

Hindus are crossing over every year. Very interesting! This could be a good story.

"Look Rahul, in 1941 Hindus made up 29.7 per cent of the population. In 1951 this decreased to 23.1 percent. After another ten years it came down to 19.6. In 1974 the Hindu population decreased to 14.6 percent. In 1981 it decreased to 13.4 percent. Every year it is going down. But in the fiveyear period between 1996 and 2001 when the Awami League was in power, the rate of migration had come down. It was not that migration had stopped altogether."

"Why do you think it had come down?" Rahul asked.

The Awami League was not able to give the Hindus anything substantial. But it certainly gave them a sense of peace. The Hindus were thinking of staying on in this country. The Awami League made them feel secure. I can tell you about an apartment house in Dhaka. This was constructed in 1990. From '90 to '96 the flats in it were owned only by Muslims, that is, all except one. This flat was owned by a Buddhist. However in '97 when nineteen new flats were added, sixteen were bought by Hindus. Many such examples can be given. Let's leave all this idle talk. It's time to have dinner and go to bed."

Two

Before leaving Delhi, the editor had briefed Rahul to give weightage to election related news. There was no need to give much heed to anything else. There was no need to write about issues related to majorities and minorities. That is why he was trying not to do a story of atrocities on Hindus despite being told about it so many times. Not only this, he himself had seen Hindu women stopped from entering the polling booth at Nazneen School in Raja Bazar, and turned away after indelible ink was put on their finger on the verandah of the school. He had seen the same thing at the polling booth in the Kamlapur High School. But he had not mentioned these things in his copy, keeping in mind the editor's briefing. After hearing what Bari had to say, he lay in his cabin and wondered whether he had made a mistake by not reporting all this. He had no work in Bhola except visiting his ancestral house. Rahul asked himself whether he should accompany Bari . He might be able to see and find out things which would be impossible to access on his own. Anyway, he would take a decision once they reached Bhola. Right now he must try and get some sleep.

Rahul turned on his side and dozed off while thinking of his wife and daughter in Delhi.

By the time he woke up, it was broad daylight but the steamer had not yet reached Bhola. It was moving towards Bhola through a narrow stream. On both sides of the stream there were rows of *Hogla* trees. Rahul went out of his cabin and knocked on Bari's door. From the bathroom, Bari said in a loud voice, "We shall reach Bhola in another twenty minutes. You should get ready. Rahul came back to his own cabin and lit a cigarette. He took out his shaving kit and went to the bathroom. When he got ready and opened his door, he saw that Bari was already there, leaning against the railing. The steamer was casting anchor on the Bhola Ghat. When the steamer was steady with the support of the pontoon, Bari said, "Come, let's get off."

"Yes, let us go."

They got off the steamer, crossed the pontoon and took a rickshaw. Rahul had already told Bari in detail about his ancestral house. The rickshaw puller set off according to the directions given by Bari. According to Rahul's father their ancestral house was outside the main city. But the rickshaw was going towards what seemed to be the town. Bari had come to Bhola earlier and was quite familiar with this small town. He had stopped the rickshaw on the way and found out the exact location of Rahul's ancestral house.

The rickshaw stopped right there. There was a big mosque next door and a pond in front of it. The sides of the pond were paved with stone. One could make out that the sides had been freshly plastered. Rahul went and sat on the side of the pond. He was not touched deeply. He did not feel either good or bad. Anyway he decided not to take a photograph. He could always tell his father that he had not been able to visit Bhola because of his hectic schedule. He scooped up a handful of earth and tied it up in his handkerchief. Then he put it in his bag and told Bari,"Let us go."

Bari did not answer. He sensed what Rahul must be feeling. He got on to the rickshaw and told the puller to take them to the Press Club.

The Press Club was deserted at that early hour. Even the peon was still asleep and had to be woken up. He was a little annoyed at being woken up.

"Whom do you want to meet?" He asked in a grumpy voice.

"No one. We just want to make a call." Bari said.

"Whom do you want to ring up?" The peon asked again.

Bari told his the name of his correspondent in Bhola.

The young boy's irritation vanished. "You want to ring up the Secretary Saheb! Come in, come in." Within fifteen minutes of the call Bari's Bhola correspondent reached the Press Club. Bari introduced Rahul to him. Rahul shook hands with him but did not reveal his complete identity. Bari's correspondent said that his name was Vilayat Hussain Kajal. He was known as Kajal here. He knew that they were coming.

While they were having breakfast at Kajal's house, Bari asked

Rahul, "Would you like to accompany us or go back?"

Without any preface Rahul said, "Let me accompany you the first day. Then I'll decide what to do."

Three

Kajal had already made arrangements for their stay. They set off on two motorcycles. Rahul was on the pillion of Kajal's motorcycle and Bari was behind Anees. Anees was not a journalist, he worked for a NGO which had asked for a report about Bhola from Dhaka. Bari liked Anees a lot after exchanging a few words with him. Today all of them were supposed to visit a village under the jurisdiction of the Lalmohan Thana in Bhola. They heard about this village for the first time from Anees. This village called Lord Hardinge was named after an English official. The official had been so happy at having a village named after him that he had arranged for more territory to be settled in his name. This was the village they were going to. Anees had been there a few days earlier and was familiar with the route though it was quite far from the town of Bhola. The others were going there for the first time. Suddenly Bari's mobile phone rang and they had to stop. It was a call for Rahul. Before leaving Dhaka he had left Bari's mobile number at the hotel with instructions that if there was a call from Delhi, the caller should be asked to ring up this number. It was a call from Rahul's editor who spoke in a loud voice. Rahul asked why he had rung up so early in the morning.

Editor: "About thirty thousand Hindus have crossed over to West Bengal after the elections. Some have gone to Tripura. All of them talk of atrocities on Hindus. I have heard that this is going on. Why don't you do a story on this?"

Rahul: "You had briefed me not to take up the Hindu-Muslim issue. Moreover…"

Editor: "I take back my briefing at once. Any other thing?"

Rahul:" What about my visa etc.?"

Editor: "I shall arrange all that. Have you received the money?"

Rahul: "Yes, yesterday."

Editor: "Do a story on the atrocities on Hindus after proper investigations and talking to people on both sides. If necessary visit the spot. Send the story tomorrow."

Rahul: "I shall send the first story by eight thirty this evening. Complete the posting only after checking the mail."

Editor: "If nothing major happens in India, your story will be the lead article. Today the Northern Alliance has captured Kabul-Kandhar but I will give your story more weightage. I shall wait for it. " Saying this the editor hung up.

Rahul was talking to his editor in English with Hindi words thrown in. Most persons in Bangladesh could understand Hindi now, even speak it a bit because of Hindi films and satellite.

Rahul did not know this. Bari started laughing as Rahul returned the mobile. Rahul looked at him inquiringly, not comprehending.

Bari: "So you have to stay on in Bhola."

Rahul:" So it seems."

Bari:" A few days before the eighth General Elections atrocities were committed on Hindus in various parts of the country. Even people in this country are not fully aware of the extent of these atrocities. It is still carrying on. We believe that at least a thousand women of various age groups have been gang raped. After the freedom struggle there has not been such large scale atrocities on Hindus so far. This is what one can say from what we have heard."

Rahul:" Who is behind this? What do you feel?"

Bari: "The powers that lost the Elections in '71 are now the partners of the party in power. So, they are completing the work which was left unfinished in '71 in a well planned manner. They want to rid this country of Hindus. Those who might stay on after such large scale atrocities, will be a handful. This is to make sure that there is no Hindu factor in the next elections. These are the people who plan to bring down the number of Hindus, as they have done in Pakistan."

Rahul:" What is the police doing?"

Bari:" Looking on without saying anything. In some places even helping the rapists. The police will act according to the orders of their superiors."

Anees interrupted, saying, "We have to go a long way. We have to talk to the victims on the spot too. This conversation can be carried on even in the evening." So they continued their journey without.

By the time they reached Lord Hardinge, it was noon. Anees said that they had to go further. The village they were going to visit was called Char Annada Prasad. It was part of the Lord Hardinge Union. He also said that the road was not safe. No one said anything. As they entered the village, they were stopped by the police who wanted to know their identity. As Bari showed his press card, the havaldar told them with a show of politeness to leave their motorcycles at the camp and proceed on foot. If need be an escort could be provided. Bari realized that this was a matter of security and told him, "You can keep our motorcycles. But there is no need for any of you to accompany us."

There were about four hundred houses of Hindus in this village. The day after the elections notorious people with political connections had attacked their houses at night after taking out processions, distributing sweets and celebrating their victory in various ways. The Hindu families had anticipated such an attack and had sent about a hundred women to the 'Dendar Ghar' which was considered the safest place in the village. The owner of this was a Hindu but he was respected by both Hindus and MuslimsThe attackers looted all the Hindu houses and finally barged into the 'Dendar Ghar'They divided themselves into ten groups to destroy, loot, even set fire to Hindu houses. Most of the Hindus in this village were affluent and it took some time for the booty to be divided. As the 'Dendar Ghar' was attacked, fifty women who had taken shelter there tried desperately to save themselves. Some jumped into the water in the nearby rice fields but the attackers compelled them to come out threatening to drown their children otherwise. No one who had taken refuge there could save herself. Whether it was an eight year old girl or a sixty five year old woman, no one escaped the attackers and all were raped and tortured throughout the night. A woman called Parulbala Saha was attacked by thirty eight leeches as she jumped into the water but she dared not come out. Mizan and Salim whom she looked upon as her younger brothers, pulled her out of the water and raped her. Parulbala showed Bari and Rahul the black marks on her body where the leeches had stuck to her. As she talked about the rape, she started sobbing, hiding her face in her sari. Rahul did not know how to comfort her. He had never come across such brutality before. Even Bari was at a loss for words. Kajal looked on silently. Tears streamed out of Anees' eyes.

Twelve years back, Shefali Rani Das had slipped and fallen while fetching water from the pond. Wrong treatment on the part of village doctor led to gangrene. The leg of this woman had to be amputated from the knee. For twelve years this woman had been looking after her family and two children, limping around on one leg. When the militants attacked the village on the night after the election, she wanted to save herself by hiding in knee-deep water. But her crutch slipped when she was getting into the water and she fell. The crutch floated away from her. Helplessly she watched it moving away from her. When she could not catch hold of the crutch which had been a support to her for twelve years, she got out of the water somehow with the help of both hands and a foot and hid herself in the turmeric field nearby. From there she could see her home which she had set up over a period of twenty years being looted. She had come to this village at the age of sixteen. Within three years of her marriage, her mother-in-law had passed away. Since then she had been looking after her home. She could not stop herself from crying out when she saw the attackers breaking the images in her Puja room. This drew them towards her They dragged her towards the tree where they had hidden their loot. Then they raped her one by one. She could remember seven of them, after which she fainted.

The adjoining village was called Jahajmara. A little boy called Sangram lived here. His name has a history. He was born on the night of 2 October when there was no one in the house except Jayanti's old mother-in-law and an old midwife. The terrorists attacked the house when Jayanti was having labour pains. The midwife ran out of the back door. Only the helpless Jayanti and her mother-in-law were left in the house. When the militants tried to break open the door with knives and daggers, Sangram was born. Muktirani, Jayanti's moterh-in-law wrapped the newborn and the mother tightly in a sari and escaped through the back door so that they could be saved. In fact Muktirani had not even managed to sever the umbilical cord. She did it at night when they had got to a safe place under a tree. It was she who named the baby Sangram. After the freedom struggle when Bangladesh became independent, many had given names like 'Sangram', 'Mukti', 'Jay' 'Durjay' to their children. But what kind of a freedom fight was this? Thirty years after the country's independence, the Hindus of Annadaprasad, Jahajmara and the whole of Bangladesh were facing the problems that they had faced earlier. Even now a newborn child was named Sangram because of the prevailing situation.

The Hindus of Jahajmara village had paid sixty thousand Taka to Jahangir Mastan for their safety. But the terrorists were not happy with this. They wanted donation on a daily, weekly or monthly basis. The inhabitants of Jahajmara village formed a committee to save themselves from the attackers. It was resolved that this committee would collect donations from Hindus and arrange for sixty thousand rupees to be paid every month. Every month the money had to be paid to Mastan as he was the local leader of the ruling party and the leader of the gang of terrorists. Those people had threatened that if the money stopped coming, there would be another attack on the village. The terrorists had also said that if all the Hindus in the village embraced Islam, started eating meat, went to the mosque five times for *namaz* they would not have to pay a single penny. There was another option. If the Hindus left the village, they would not have to pay any money provided that they did not sell even a small piece of their land. If they wanted to go on living in Jahajmara as Hindus, they would have to pay sixty thousand Taka every month. Dr Ramakrishna Bose ventured to ask,"How long do we have to pay the money ?" "As long as we remain in power." The *mamun* or leader of the gang had replied arrogantly. Dr Ramakrishna did not dare to ask why *Mamun's* gang had looted his dispensary in Gajariya Bazar, taken down the signboard and put up another signboard saying 'Durjay Sports Club" in its place. They had taken over his dispensary and made it a club, their *adda*.

After visiting Annadaprasad and Jahajmara villages with his companions, Rahul returned to Bhola to Anees' office, at about eight in the evening. Kajal had already said that email facilities were available here. Rahul would email his copy to Delhi and Bari would fax his. But Bari had to compose his story. Both sat down at the computer. Rahul would consult sometimes Rahul wrote a long story based on his visit to Annadaprasad and Jahajmara, and the information that he had received from Bari. Along with the case study of Annadaprasad and Jahajmari villages, he wrote that the Hindus of Bangladesh were being compelled to leave the land of their forefathers, their birthplace, ancestral homes where their parents had passed away along with the memories of their childhood and happier times spent here. Even tears that flow uncontrollably on such occasions, had to be shed in secret. Only someone who has experienced something like this would know how much it hurts.The tragedy was that if there were people who sympathized with the Hindus who were going away, their numbers might go down. No Hindu was able to achieve much after going to India, specially after Bangladesh became independent. Of course those who had something to look forward to in Kolkata before independence was different. Actually, the riots that shook Noakhali in October 1946 had created a sense of insecurity among Hindus. That was the beginning of migration. After the partition of the country, there was a fear as the powers that be had not made any constitutional changes. This increased the number of migrants to India. The Pakistani rulers discriminated between Hindus and Muslims. This discrimination led to a high rate of migration – about eleven lakhs in the first six months. The migrants were mostly from the middle class and a large number of them(about a lakh) were farmers. The number of labourers was a little below a lakh and the rest belonged to the upper class-landlords and others. Those left behind were the real targets of the fundamentalists. Whenever attempts were made to make this country a democratic state whenever progressive people united to fight the satanic forces, communal frenzy, communal attacks and well organized communal atrocities were used as a trump cad by the fundamentalist forces. Hindus were insecure because the progressive forces were weakened. This situation occurred in the country not once but many times. The atrocities that had been committed in the country when it was a part of Pakistan, continued even in independent Bangladesh. The same chain of events had occurred this time-attacks on Hindus, rape of Hindu women etc. All this had become normal in this part of the world.

Rahul read the whole story once. The editor himself was awaiting it. Then they went to Kajal's house , had a wash and sat down to dinner. Bari's phone rang. He looked at the number and handed the phone to Rahul.The editor thanked Rahul and said,"I want to publish an article with detailed description of the atrocities on Hindus. You will have to visit different areas and send me a story every day. It will be published in a series, starting from tomorrow." The editor added, "Today I have given an order for ten thousand extra copies" Rahul said that he would arrange to send a story every day and rang off.

Four

All four of them set out on two motorcycles as on the previous day. Today they had started very early, even before sunrise. They had decided to breakfast on the way, in Daulatkhan Bazar. After visiting the spot there, they were to visit Umedchar village in the Lalmohan district. Their first halt was at Lejpata village near Daulatkhan. Anees brought them here for the first time. There were thirteen Hindu families living here. None of the men had even a shirt on. All of them were wearing new *gamchhas*. The terrorists had taken everything away, even the clothes that they had worn. The night following the elections, all this had happened when they were sleeping. A gang of twenty five to thirty men came and burst a bomb. The sound woke everyone up. The attackers shouted slogans like '*Nara-e-Taqbeer Allah Ho Akbar*, Prabharani Devi, Pareshnath Mistry's wife told them. She ran out of the back door and jumped into the pond to save herself. But the fundamentalists managed to locate her with the help of a torch, caught hold of her hair and pulled her out. They gang raped her and even pulled off the nose ring that she had on. As she narrated all this Prabharani started sobbing helplessly. Four young girls of the neighbourhood – Beena, Pali, Milan and Shipra tried to hide in the *Hogla* bushes nearby, but could not save themselves. She pointed to a five year old girl called Rinku whose nose ring was ripped off tearing the skin. The fundamentalists had come prepared to loot with vans and rickshaws. After stripping young girls in front of helpless parents and wives in front of husbands, they raped them and beat up all the men with hockey sticks. They took away everything from these thirteen houses-luggage, bedding, clothes even the foodgrain that that they could find .There were three cows in the neighbourhood which were not spared.

From here Rahul and his companions went to the house of Anjurani, member of the Charpata Union. One day before the polling, a group of masked young men had come and warned them against going to vote. From that time they were very scared. Four days earlier, a television set and other things had been looted from Anjurani's house. A fortnight back her bodyguard had been murdered. Nityahari Ray, a member of Anjurani's office told Rahul and his friends all this. An old woman called Pushpanjali Hawladar from the Hawladar family said that their house and the *supari* orchard had ben looted. For the last five years there had been no sense of fear here. But the day after the elections, all the leaders of the Awami League from this village ran away. If they had remained here these crimes might have averted.

The young Hindu girls of Charduari village had been criminally assaulted repeatedly and they had gone mad as a result. They lived with the doors of their houses wide open. Not only this, one of them had written outside her house 'do whatever you want'. Rahul and his companions did not have the courage to talk to these distraught women. Bari did want to talk to them, but Anees stopped him. He had been here before. As soon as these women saw a man approaching, they would take off their clothes. The extent of atrocities committed on them again and again, had unhinged them. For them every man was a potential rapist.

Noorjahan Begum was walking as if in a frenzy. Rahul and his companions stopped their motorcycles to talk to her. As soon as learnt that they were journalists, she begged them not to publish anything that she told them, or else she would be murdered. She worked at the house of Asitbala who had paid twelve thousand Taka to save herself from the fundamentalists. But they had told her not to breathe a word of it to anyone or else...Every year this family celebrated Durga Puja on a grand scale, but this year the Puja pandal was empty. A dog was crying outside the pandal. Asitbala might have saved herself by paying twelve thousand Taka but the others in her family were not safe. Even before the elections she had sent all the girls to Mirzakalu to their in-laws house. Noorjahan used to cook for them. Asitbala might have saved herself but not Noorjahan. She went mad and roamed about the streets. When she met journalists, she would plead with them not to write anything about her as that would make them kill her.

Anees told them that they would visit Charkumari village

shortly. Nepal Ray, a middle aged resident of the village, fainted as he recounted what had happened on 2 October, the day after the elections. He was sitting in the Kolhu in the village, telling Rahul and his companions what had happened. Farid Khalifa, a religious man who was respected by all in the village, came and said that he apprehended trouble. He added that if things were looted they could be replaced but the honour of women could not be restored if they were molested. Nepal Ray and his family had a lot of faith in Farid Khalifa. When he talked in that manner, there was no reason to disbelieve him.

Nepal asked him, "What can we do?"

Farid answered, "Send the womenfolk to some distant place, to some relative."

Nepal said, "But it is quite late now. Your party has won the elections. Please tell them not to harm us"

Farid retorted in an irritated manner, "I don't know the persons who might attack. I have only heard that there might be an attack. You could do one thing. You could send all the women to my bungalow for the night."

Nepal agreed immediately in good faith. He would be eternally grateful to Farid Khalifa for providing shelter to thirty-thirty five women this night. Early tomorrow he would send his wife, daughter and widowed sister to a relative's house far away from this troubled area. The others decided to do the same thing. Farid Khalifa had told him to send the women to his house after the *namaz.* Nepal did just that. Thirty-thirty five women, some sleeping, others thinking about their homes in the darkness, were biding their time in Farid's bungalow. Just then he called out to them from outside. They ignored the first two calls. But when he knocked for the third time, one of them got up and opened the door. This was Nepal Ray's daughter, a young girl studying in class nine. Farid flashed a torch on her face, on her entire body and then the room. The next instant he threw it away and gestured to some people to enter the room. A horde of men rushed into the room. Farid had gripped the hand of Nepal Ray's daughter with one hand. With the other, he closed the door as soon as the hooligans had entered. Then he told one of the men to light a lantern. He took out a dagger and told the women that if any of them dared to cry for help he would slit her throat. After that he dragged Nepal Ray's daughter to one corner of the room. From twelve at night to three in the morning, the women were raped bestially. When Nepal Ray's daughter fainted, Farid called out to her mother. When Savita saw her daughter covered with blood, she rushed to take her in her arms, but Farid pushed her and she fell flat by her daughter's side. Nepal Ray could not get on with the story, he had fainted.

Rahul and his friends could not go to the Charumed village in the Lalmohan sub-district. It was getting late and going there would mean that they would not be able to send in their reports for the day. They returned to Bhola and went straight to Anees' office. Bari sat down to type out his report on the Bengali typewriter while Rahul worked on his in English asking Bari questions now and then. Bari presented a living history of Bangladesh, a nightmarish one at that. Rahul knew that if he had come to Bhola with anyone elsei, his story would not have been so authentic.

Though General Zia ur Rahman had been a *Muktiyoddha* or freedom fighter himself, after he came to power, there was a rise in communal fundamentalism in Bangladesh. His Prime Minister was a fundamentalist *Razakar* who was opposed to freedom. During Zia's regime, the notion of secularism was deleted from the Constitution and communalism was ushered in as an integral part of governance. The seeds of communalism and fundamentalism sown by General Zia were well nurtured by General Ershad after him. In the history of Bangladesh General Ershad was the only ruler who encouraged communalism so much and used it to his own benefit. During his regime about thirty six lakh Hindus crossed over to India. It must be remembered that this was triggered off by the terrible communal riots of 1990. During the regime of Khaleda Zia, the atrocities that were inflicted on Hindus on the basis of the demolition of the Babri Masjid in Ayoddha, are beyond words. About twenty eight thousand houses belonging to Hindus were demolished, two thousand and seven hundred shops and commercial premises destroyed totally. Three thousand and six hundred temples and places of worship were razed and torched to avenge the demolition of the Babri Masjid. About twelve Hindus were killed and two thousand injured. About two thousand and six hundred Hindu women were assaulted. The total financial loss was over two hundred crores of Taka. In this country Hindu women were no longer safe as a section of the Muslims considered them easy prey. Though there was no law like the one that allowed takeover of property that had been left behind by Hindus, the fundamentalists considered it their right to rape Hindu women just to show their superiority. After Bangladesh became free, Sheikh Mujibur Rahman had governed the country on the basis of a secular Constitution. Sheikh Hasina had done away with the vested Property Law in her five year tenure. Hindus were not discriminated against .It can be said that during these nine years Hindus in Bangladesh had lived happily. Though the Constitution of Bangladesh does not say specifically that a non-Muslim cannot become the President, the word *Bismillah* at the beginning is significant. It is thought that no one except a Muslim will be able to justice to the concept of *Bismillah* . Even if this is not considered, no Hindu can dream of becoming the President of a country with such a Constitution.

This was Rahul's report.

Tiredly, Rahul slumped on a cot in Kajal's house. Bari was lying on the cot next to him. Suddenly Bari's mobile rang. He gave it to Rahul after checking the number. It was a call from his editor in Delhi. He thanked Rahul for the story he had just sent and told him not to send any more stories about Bhola. He was instructed to find out about other places where atrocities had been committed against Hindus and return to Dhaka the next day. The editor also told him to find out the reactions to these atrocities in Dhaka and do a story on that. He rang off before Rahul could say anything. Rahul did not know how he could reach Dhaka the next day. He called Kajal and asked whether it would be possible to get a steamer to Dhaka that night. He looked at Bari helplessly when Kajal answered in the negative. Bari reassured him. He could go to Barisal from here and then catch a flight to Dhaka. He would reach Dhaka in the afternoon, Bari said. Bari himself would stop at Bhola for a few days more.

[illegible] Property [illegible]

[illegible]

[illegible]

[illegible]

[illegible]

Five

Rahul reached Dhaka before the scheduled time but there was no time to collect information for his story. When he reached the hotel, it struck him that he could write his story only after he had read all that had been published in the local newspapers about the atrocities on Hindus. White House, the hotel in Shantinagar that he was staying in, was quite close to the office of *Jankanth*, a national daily. He decided to go there and took an auto. Stringent security measures had been adopted by the office of this newspaper after terrorists had left a briefcase there with bombs in it. Rahul was frisked and searched with the help of a metal detector before being permitted to go in. Once the formalities at the reception were complete he was allowed to go up to the eighth floor where the editors sat. He sent his card in and waited. He was called in after some time. When he told the editor the purpose of his visit, the latter sent him to the library in the adjoining room with a peon. Here Rahul looked through the English and Bangla newspapers to assess the way in which the Elections had been covered. The headline "Stop atrocities on minorities: President orders" caught his attention. He read the entire story, made notes and turned the pages. "Humanity under attack, save minorities: Thousand of students appeal". Another headline! He read this also and took notes. "Stop atrocities on minorities: European Commission". He read this carefully and took down the relevant points. The papers carried many features by progressive persons which he read. He noted down the title of the feature by the well known poet Shamsur Rehman. The feature with the title "Victory to Humanity and Welfare" attracted him and he took down a few lines so that he could quote them. The column with letters to the editor in *Prothom Alo* caught his attention. Eleven letters were published under the heading "Please cancel our right to vote". A photograph of a middle aged woman wiping her tears while her husband stood by her side pointing to his wounds. The caption said "A victimised family from the minority section". Rahul selected portions from one of the eleven letters. It was anonymous, perhaps the writer had not dared to give his/her name. It only said – a citizen from the minority community.' The letter from Magura said, "Can we call ourselves Bengalis? Would that be proper? Do we really have a racial identity? It is the duty of the Government to provide security to its citizens, irrespective of race. Why are we deprived of it?" Rahul took down this section from the letter. The report of students from Dhaka University students going on strike and hunger strike to protest against atrocities on minority communities struck him as rather significant. He noted down names of organizations like Mahila Parishad, Grip Trust, Nari Pragati Sangh and others. Representatives from these NGOs had visited different parts of the country and collected data on the atrocities on Hindus which they had had presented at the press conference. Several organizations in Dhaka had formed a human chain as a mark of protest against communal ravages. By the time Rahul had noted it down, it was past eight, it would be seven thirty in Delhi. He put the files of newspapers aside and came out. His destination was the familiar cyber café in the Rajmani Isa Khan Complex. He suddenly remembered that he had not checked his email for five days. As he clicked his yahoo.com ID, he got some more info from it. AP, the American news agency had circulated a news item and a photograph with the caption "Supporters of Right Wing Islamic Fundamentalist Bangladesh Nationalist Party, BNP Celebrate in Dhaka". Rahul scanned the photograph along with the caption.

He wrote a covering letter to his editor telling him about his arrival in Dhaka and the way in which he had collected material for his story. Then he started on his story. In between he went out for a smoke. As he was going back to his story after his smoke, the manager who knew him, placed a copy of the weekly supplement of *Prothom Alo*, a daily, before him. But he just did not have the time to look at it. It was not possible to look at anything else till he was through with the story. So he took the supplement against his wishes. The manager had marked a certain page for him. This had a number of short news about the ways in which Hindus were being tortured. One of them attracted his attention. The heading said "Electro Cardiography Show".

He included this in the story that he was going to send. In Barisal the militants could not find Sudhir, so they robbed his house. While going they took away the sari that his wife was wearing. Nitai Seal, a resident of Hijla thana area could not meet his mother who was on deathbed. He could not even be present at her cremation. What was his crime? Was it that he as a Hindu?A hundred years back William Anthavan from Holland had invented the Electro Cardiograph, a machine that could scan the movements inside the human heart and display it on its screen. It would not be a bad idea to arrange an Electro Cardiography Show to show all the painful movements in the hearts of these oppressed and unhappy people.

Rahul included some sections of another news item in his story. BNP workers attacked the house of Ranjit Mandal, a college lecturer from Faridpur. After taking away what they considered valuable, they destroyed everything and beat up women and old men. The Shitala temple in Hasnadia village was set on fire. On their way back, the militants slaughtered two cows that belonged to Ranjit Mandal and divided up the meat amongst themselves. We feel that they should have slaughtered a few more cows with government help to feed themselves for five years.

Rahul cited from this news as well. Today his story had become quite long. He wanted to read it once before sending it off. But it was already nine thirty. So he sent a message saying that he was sending his story in thirty minutes. He sent the picture and its caption that he had got from Yahoo.com and read his story once. He added one more paragraph and read it again. He added the note about razing of temples and images that he had compiled from different newspapers. He added the news about breaking of images at Palashbari Gaibanda and acts of arson at the Puja pandal at Bauphal in Patuakhali. He also included the news about teachers in Dhaka University taking out a silent procession as a mark of protest against all that was happening. Though the Government had denied that atrocities had been committed on Hindus, the intellectuals supporting the ruling party had spoken against all that was happening. He mentioned the names of the intellectuals of the BNP who had spoken out. By the time he finished the story, there were twelve minutes to ten. As he pressed the 'send' button, he realized that it would be almost nine thirty in Delhi now. Though it was quite late, Rahul was satisfied with the story he had just sent. He went to the Kakrail corner and lit a cigarette feeling lighter. He was in the mood to chat with the rickshaw puller.

"What is your name?"

"Abdul Malik."

"Are you from Dhaka?"

"No, Comilla."

"Where did you cast your vote?"

"In Comilla."

"How did the elections go this time?"

"Very well Awami League had turned our country into another India. Now that BNP is in power we feel free once again."

"Is that so…" Rahul sounded curious.

"Of course. Don't you think so?" the rickshaw puller retorted. Then he turned and asked, "Whom did you vote for?"

"I did not vote."

"Why, were you away?"

"No. Rahul's reply was monosyllabic.

Rahul kept quiet for a while. Then he asked, "You said that the country has become free once again."

"Yes sir."

"How so?"

"When the Awami League was in power for five years the country was teeming with Hindus. That was inevitable. After all, the Awami League is a party of Hindus.I have heard that Sheikh Mujib's father was a Hindu."

"Is that so? Who told you?"

"Our MP mentioned it in his speech. It is written in small leaflets also."

"What kind of leaflets?"

The rickshaw puller stopped his vehicle on one side of the road and asked Rahul to get off, very politely. Then he lifted the seat, took out a leaflet and proffered it to Rahul. As he read it under the street light, Rahul was stunned. How can a country call someone Father of the Nation and then spread such filth about him, he asked himself. Then he told Malik the rickshaw puller, "What this leaflet says is not true. It's totally false."

"How can the written word be false, sir?"

"Why not, anything whether true or false, can be written down. It just reveals the mentality of the writer and shows how mean one can be."

"All right, tell me one thing. If Sheikh Mujib had not been a Hindu, what made the Hindus vote for his party?"

"Voting is a matter of one's likes and dislikes. What has that to do with the Hindu-Muslim question?"

"This time the Hindus have been taught a lesson they will not forget in a hurry." Malik said.

"By whom?"

"I realize sir that you know nothing. I am an illiterate man, can't read newspapers or anything else for that matter. But it is common knowledge that Hindus have been beaten up badly. Even their women have not been spared."

"Do you know who is doing all this?"

"The leaders of the Awami League and BNP are blaming each other."

"What do you think? After all you voted for the BNP?"

"You are absolutely right sir. How did you know that I voted for the BNP, on the grain of rice?"

"From your words."

"Okay. You asked me who had organized all this violence. Though I voted for the BNP, I am not a blind supporter of the party. I have always voted for the BNP and will do so in future. But the fact is that after the elections the Awami leaders are on the run, trying to save their own skins. How can they kill Hindus or even rob them? They wouldn't even have the time to molest Hindu women. I am sure all this is being done by the BNP boys."

By this time the rickshaw had reached the hotel. Rahul paid the fare and went in. He wished that he could convey what Abdul Malik had said to the Home Minister of this country. They were just not prepared to accept the fact that Hindus were being hounded in this country. They believed that it was the work of the Awami League in order to discredit the BNP and gain political mileage out of it. But one cannot always do everything that one wants to. After all Rahul was only a foreign correspondent here. Though he could speak in Bangla that did not make him a citizen of Bangladesh. What difference did it make that his forefathers were from Bhola and the ruins of his ancestral house were there. . But the thought continued to nag him though he tried to shake it off. He wondered how his father would have reacted if he had seen a mosque in place of his ancestral house. Would he have tolerated it?

Rahul went to his room and started planning his assignment for the next day. He rang up Shyamal from *Bhorer Kagoj*. Shyamal told him that a rape victim from Mahakhali had agreed to address a press conference the next day. An NGO from Dhaka had brought her here from Sirajganj.

Rahul asked if the girl had revealed her name.

"Yes," Shyamal had answered.

"What is her name?" Rahul asked.

"Purnimarani Sil."

Six

The river Muktahar which often devastates the district of Sirajganj, was at peace now and winding its way slowly. On the western bank of the river there was a village called Purab Delua in Ullapara. Some people call it Bhootgachha. The Asian Highway passes through the middle of the village and goes all the way from Nagarbari to Dinajpur. A narrow track took one from the highway to Anil Sil's house. He had five sons and four daughters. Purnimarani was the youngest. She studied in class ten in the Eastern Delua High School. In December and was not yet sixteen. Eight days after the Elections Anil Seal was sleeping with his family in his house. At midnight his wife was woken up by a loud hammering on their door. She shook her husband who was in deep sleep. He could hear screams coming from the other rooms. As he went to investigate, the door broke open with a sudden bang and many armed men barged into the house. As the Seals watched, stunned, the entire was robbed in a matter of minutes. Suddenly she remembered Purnima. As she rushed towards the door she saw some of the intruders dragging her away. She tried to stop them but was pushed aside brutally. She fell down, picked herself up and again tried to go to her daughter's rescue. This time she was hit on the head and lost consciousness. As she recounted all this at the press conference, she wiped the tears that streamed down her face. Firdausi Priyadarshini had her arm round her and was trying to console her. During the Bangladesh Liberation Struggle, Pakistani soldiers had captured Firdausi and committed atrocities on her for quite a few days. After Bangladesh became independent, women like her who had been tortured by Pakistani soldiers were honoured with awards of bravery. She had been one of them. She was not trying to console Basanarani Seal. After Basana had had her say, Purnima was given the mike. The press conference had been organized by the Committee that had been formed in 1971 to fight murderous reactionary agents.

Shyamali Nasreen Chaudhury was sitting next to Purnima, on her right. Her husband, Dr. Alim Chaudhury, a well known eye specialist, had been abducted from his own house in Dhaka in '71 by Pakistani soldiers. His whereabouts were still not known. They had not been able to identify any of them except one. This was Maulana Mannan who had led the soldiers to their house. After Bangladesh gained freedom Mannan was absconding, but that did not prevent Zia ur Rahman from making him a minister in his cabinet. Even General Ershad made him a minister as soon as he came into power. Later Mannan embezzled money meant for teachers at madarasa and started his own newspaper which he called *Inquilab*. This was the most fundamentalist newspaper in Bangladesh.

On the other side of Purnima sat Aroma Datta the granddaughter of Dhirendranath Datta who had sacrificed his life for the country. It was Dhirendranath Datta who had raised the issue that Bangla should be the national language for the first time in the parliament. This was how the historical movement of twenty first February started in 1952. The next step was a demand for an independent Bangladesh which led to the freedom in the country in 1971.When a call was given for the freedom struggle to begin, Dhirendranath Datta was at home in Comilla. The Pakistani soldiers arrested him and subjected him to inhuman tortures in military jail as long as he was alive. His knees were broken, his eyes were gouged out. Not only did his body bear marks of torture, there were deep wounds where his flesh had been carved out. A Bengali barber working at the military camp had been an eye witness to all this

Purnima had never used the microphone before this. She had not come here in normal circumstances today. The fifteen year old girl was supposed to recount a nightmarish experience that had shattered her life, in public. Eighth of October had been the darkest night of her life. Purnima knew that a rape victim had no respect in society. Either people laughed at her or showed hollow sympathy or even contempt. Rapists were men and patriarchal society condoned them most of the time. But Purnima was determined to expose the men who had assaulted her and this gave her courage. But she could not control herself while talking about that dreadful night and started sobbing . Not a single eye in the hall was dry. A crying Shyamali Nasreen

Chaudhary put her arms round her. Even Rahul could not control his tears when Purnima spoke about the way in which about thirty people forced themselves on poor Purnima one after another. For two hours the poor girl had to put up with this. No one bothered to find out whether she was alive or dead. When members of her family finally managed to locate her lying unconscious, they found unused condoms lying all around. Those who had tried to stop the intruders had been beaten up mercilessly. The marks were there for all to see.

Rahul sent a news story to his paper based on what he had heard at Purnima's press conference, that very evening. He also informed the Delhi office that he would be sending another story later. After coming back to his hotel, he spread out the map of Bangladesh on his bed. He had managed to procure it that very day. An NGO with the name of Prip Trust had issued this map which was of four colours. This map provided statistics regarding the areas where atrocities were committed on Hindus even before the Elections. The NGO had conducted surveys as to the degree of atrocities and Bhola, Barisal and Bagerhat had been pinpointed as areas where Hindus had suffered the most. These areas had been marked out in the map as 'the most seriously affected areas'. Chittagong, Sirajganj, Pabna, Rajshahi and Patuakhali came in 'seriously affected areas' and 'affected areas' included Natore, Gajipur, Feni, Jhinaidhah, Lalmonir Hat, Gopalganj, Satkhira and Meherpur districts. In a nutshell out of sixty four districts in the country, fifty nine had been marked as districts where Hindus had been exploited in various ways. Rahul thought of writing another story on the basis of the information provided by the map. After the demolition of the Babri Masjid in Ayodhya, there were many communal riots in Bangladesh, and the fundamentalists tried to destroy the Hindus altogether. But this time the attacks and atrocities were mainly on Hindus living in villages. Of course there were sporadic incidents in cities and towns but nothing compared to what happened in rural areas. Rahul wondered whether there was any particular reason behind this. He went out of his hotel with the intention of finding out the reason behind this.

He got into a rickshaw and proceeded once again towards Rajmani Isha Khan Complex. As the rickshaw turned from Shantinagar to Kakrail, Rahul's eyes fell on a multistoreyed building. Taslima Nasreen had lived in a flat in this very building. She had bought this flat but had not been able to live here very long. She had to leave the country for raising her voice against exploitation of religious minorities, raising the question of women's rights and exposing conspiracies hatched by fundamentalists and the corruption that was rampant among them. Even while she was here, they had made life hell for her. If she had not left the country for her safety, she might have paid with her life. The fundamentalists had declared a *fatwa* against her. They had promised a hefty reward to anyone who would eliminate her.

Rahul did not know Taslima but admired her for her courage. She had said things that nobody else had dared to, though they were absolutely true. She had to pay a heavy price for telling the truth. She lost her motherland, and her fundamental rights, one by one. Her own country never gave any importance to her rights as a citizen or even as a human being. The truths that Taslima had articulated, were not really punishable, at the most she could be imprisoned for *three* years, whereas those who tried to kill her or put a price on her head could receive death sentence. But what happened ultimately? The authorities pounced upon the person who could be let off with a light punishment, but did not say a word to the fundamentalists who tried to kill her. As Rahul reached the Kakrail crossing, beyond which the rickshaw could not go, all these thoughts crossed his mind. He had to get off here and proceed to Rajmani Isa Khan Complex on foot. He did not mind the short walk. There were other considerations. Some roads in Dhaka did not allow rickshaws. These were called VIP roads But this was not the way to decongest roads. Rahul remembered the crossing which was always full of cars. If the authorities wanted to stop rickshaws from plying in order to decongest roads they should do so in the entire city. Rahul had not seen any place in Dhaka which was not full of cars. There was a time when Dhaka was known as the city of mosques. Could one call it a city full of cars now, Rahul wondered.

Rahul went to the cyber café and started composing his story. The manager placed a copy of *Prothom Alo* before him. He pointed out a letter in the 'letters to the Editor' column and asked Rahul to take a look. He remarked, "If we think like the person writing this letter, the situation in our country is bound to become peaceful and progressive. "Rahul stopped writing and read the letter. He was not familiar with the term *Shabe-Barat* and wanted to know what it meant. The manager told him that it referred to the night when God decided the destiny of all human beings for the coming year. Whatever one asked for from the Creator, was sure to be granted. The lady who had written this letter had remained awake throughout the night of *Shabe-barat* . She had offered *namaz* along with the rites that the occasion demanded, but had not been able to ask God for anything. She considered herself guilty as members of her faith had committed atrocities on Hindus. As a member of the majority community, she could not absolve herself of the guilt.

Rahul translated the entire letter and quoted it in his story. He thanked the manager and came out. He wondered whether he could go to the Press Club. On second thought he wondered whether it was a good idea as none of his acquaintances would be there at this hour. They would be at their desks, writing their stories and he would have no one to talk to. Still, he took an auto and proceeded to the Press Club. As the auto stopped at the crossing near Kakrail Masjid, he seemed to see it for the first time. He recalled that the Tablig jamaat in Bangladesh was controlled from this place. Every year there was an international conference of the Tablig Jamaat in Tongi near Dhaka. This conference was the biggest congregation of Muslims after the Haj at Mecca. Bari had told him all this one day. Rahul had wanted to know whether it was an assembly of communal fundamentalists.

"That is not true. Those taking part in the Tablig Jamaat come from villages. They are less communal." Bari had told him then.

"So, where is the den of the fundamentalists?"

"There is no special place for them. Baitul Mukarram Masjid is the place where members of the jammat-e-Islam, a political party with a communal bias, congregate. On the northern gate of this mosque, they conduct their meetings and conferences throughout the year. In fact there is a kind of conflict between the Tablig Jamaat and jamaat-e-Islam. You can say that they do not share a cordial relationship. They cannot stand each other."

Today Rahul wondered whether the members of the Tablig could be held responsible for the atrocities on Hindus as they had suffered most in the rural areas. He wanted to know why Hindus in the rural areas had been singled out for exploitation. As the signal changed, the auto proceeded towards Topkhana Road.

At the Press Club he met Afsana Chaudhary. She suggested that he come over to her place and he agreed. Earlier she had told him about her maid but he did not have the time to visit her that day. Today Rahul did not have too much on his hands and they took a rickshaw for Magbazar where Afsana lived.

At home Afsana called Jharna, her new maid to the drawing room. She hesitated to come in when she saw Rahul and entered when Afsana reassured her. Jharna came in but kept standing. She wanted to know if Rahul would like some tea. When Rahul reused tea, she requested him to stay on for dinner. Rahul smiled and said nothing. He had heard a lot about the hospitable people of Dhaka in Delhi and Kolkata. However this was the first time that someone had asked him to stay on for a meal without prior invitation. Afsana said to Jharna, "Sit down and tell Rahul all that had happened in your village. Don't feel embarrassed."

"What is your full name?"

"Jharna Basak."

"I am Rahul Roy from Delhi. Tell me what happened in your village."

"Are you a Hindu?" Jharna wanted to know.

Though Rahul did not have anything to do with religion, something that had displeased his mother, he said yes so that Jharna could speak freely. He had heard that people talked about their nightmarish experiences with Hindus only. It could be either fear or grief which did not let them talk about their plight with non-Hindus. He had heard from Bari that no one spoke to Muslims about what they had gone through. That was why he had given his full name to Jharna.

"What happened in your village?"

"What is the use talking about it now?"

"If you don't want to talk about it, I will not force you."

"No, it is all right."

"Then tell me what happened."

"What can I say? All those who had voted for the Awami League were singled out for exploitation."

"In what way?"

"They could do nothing to me. I escaped and hid behind a barn"

"What did you see from your hiding place?"

"It was a dreadful sight. When the men were physically exhausted and could not force themselves upon the women any more, they pushed up bamboo poles into them. As the women screamed with pain, they laughed loudly. When they fainted the men moved on."

"Did you recognize any of the men?"

"Why not? Hasim, Kafil, Mamun, Imran and others. There were about twenty five or thirty of them."

"Were some of the girls Muslim?"

"No, they were all Hindus. Some of them had to be operated upon to take out pieces of bamboo from their private parts. It was not even possible to take out the pieces in all the cases. In some cases the wounds got infected, I heard from others. I don't know what happened later. I went away to Dhaka with my aunt. I get to know all this when someone from my village comes for a visit."

Seven

Rahul was told that there had been a call for him when he returned to his hotel. The caller would ring again at eleven. It was twenty five minutes past eleven by the hotel clock. He did not go to his room. Sometimes a call transferred to the room line could not be heard properly. There were just five minutes to eleven in Delhi. He could have a quiet smoke in the hotel lounge. Even before he lit his second cigarette, the phone rang. By now his editor had stopped talking about an interview with the Prime Minister. He told Rahul to go to one of the three districts he had said were most affected. He had already sent a story from Bhola. The editor told him to go either of the two other districts and rang off. Rahul went to his room and tried to contact Jamal on his mobile but it was switched off. He then took his map out and had a look. Bagerhat was the place he decided to visit.

Tomorrow he would contact Jamal and work out the details of the visit in the morning.

Jamal told him that some persons from an NGO were visiting Bagerhat the next morning. They were planning to tour the south west areas of the district to assess the situation. Rahul could go with them if he wanted to. Rahul did not know where Bagerhat was and looked at the map of Bangladesh to find out the exact location. Bari had been of great help to him at Bhola. Meeting Kajal and Anees had made his task easier. If he could go to Bagerhat with like minded persons it would be wonderful. That was why he had contacted Jamal who was a correspondent of a Delhi paper on a stringer basis. Rahul had met him in Delhi last year. Rahul got ready for his Bagerhat visit and requested Jamal to work out the details.

Today he did not have much work to do. He wrote a story on the basis of what the young girl at Afsana Chaudhury's house had told him the previous evening and sent it by afternoon. He wanted to fix some appointments in the evening if possible with the Home Minister. That would help him to write another story. As he lay on his bed smoking and musing on all this, the phone rang. It was Shyamal.

"Shyamal this side.'

"From the office...."

"Yes. A friend from Lakshmi Bazar had reported an incident. If you want to investigate, please note down the address and location."

Yes, go on."

After noting down the address, Rahul wanted to know if it

was in old Dhaka.

"Yes. Just go to Sohrawaddy College and ask anyone there. He will point the house out to you. If you are not doing anything urgent, you can start right away. That would be ideal."

"When did this incident take place?" Rahul wanted to know.

"Today itself."

"Does your paper carry anything about it?"

"Not as yet. We want to send a woman reporter in a short while."

Rahul thanked him and put down the phone.

He found the house in Lakshmi Bazar quite easily. He just had to ask two or three persons and they told him which one it was. The old two storeyed house seemed deserted. He wondered what to do when he reached it. The gate was open but he could not see anyone. A cat slunk past him. Rahul looked around him and cleared his throat. A gentleman came and stood on the balcony of the second floor. Rahul wondered if the sound had brought him out. The gentleman on the balcony lit a cigarette. Maybe that is why he had come out. Rahul looked up and asked him if he could come in.

"Whom do you want to meet?" the man wanted to know.

"Anyone would do, I'm not particular."

"I don't get you."

"There is no one at the gate. Could you please come down?"

"Alright. Wait for a while."

Rahul did not to have to wait for long. The gentleman came down. Rahul gave him his card and said, "I want to ask you something. Don't get me wrong. Has there been a mishap in this house?"

Instead of answering he took Rahul inside. He made Rahul sit in the drawing room and said, "The victim you are looking for, is in hospital."

"What happened? Can you throw some light on it?"

"Why not? But I don't want the papers to publicize what happened to my daughter. You are from Delhi. I cannot keep a foreign journalist standing outside the gate while I talk to him. That is why I made you come in. I turned away all those who came before you."

"Why?" Rahul sounded curious.

"Whatever has happened cannot be reversed. What is lost cannot be brought back. My daughter's honour cannot be restored even if I become the richest person in the world."

"That is true. But how did it happen...."

"See, if you promise not to write a word, I can tell you what happened in brief. If it is published anywhere, my daughter's future is bleak. That is why I have refused to talk to journalists about this incident."

"All right. But I don't think anything will happen to her even if you talk about it."

"You cannot understand. It is not possible for you to understand."

"It's all right." Rahul did not want to argue with him.

"See, I live in this house with my wife, daughter and maid. The maid has taken leave and gone to her village as Durga Puja is approaching. I remain out of the house most of the time during the day. Many times those persons have tried to take possession of this by force. But during the regime of the Awami League they could do nothing. We were safe."

"From then till now?" Rahul interrupted.

"This time I went to the court three days after the Elections. My daughter went to college along with me. I dropped her there and went to the court. She went back home all by herself as I usually get late. Sometimes it gets dark by the time I get back. But yesterday I felt unwell and came back early. The gate of the house always remains open. But I noticed that the door was also open. The silence was eerie. I called out my daughter's name, no one answered. I called out angrily to my wife but there was no answer. I went up to the second floor and kept calling out for everyone from the doorstep. Then I came into the room where you are sitting. I noticed my wife lying unconscious near the TV. I threw away my briefcase, sat on the floor, put her head on my lap and tried to revive her. But to no avail. So I carried her to the bedroom, put her on the bed and rang for the ambulance. Then I saw something that made me numb with horror. It seemed that my heart would burst with grief. The room had been ransacked and my daughter was lying on my bed without any clothes. I just did not know what to do. When I tried to cover her nakedness with a sari, I noticed that the bed was full of blood. Her left nipple was bleeding. I wish I had died rather than be a witness to this. "The gentleman started sobbing loudly as he said this. Rahul did not know how to console him. He had never faced such a situation in his life and did not what to do. In a desperate effort to stop this person from crying, he asked, "Did you report the incident?"

"Even if I lodged a report, my daughter would still remain dishonoured. The police, law, courts, everyone is in their favour. No use fighting a case. That would put my daughter's life in danger. It is better that I leave this place after my daughter gets better, sell this ancestral house and go somewhere else. I don't even know if I will be able to sell this house. Those people had not come here only to rape my daughter. They had planned the whole thing. My daughter or my wife were incidental victims. Their target is taking possession of this house somehow."

"What will you do if you can't see this house?"

"We will leave it and go away to a safer place."

The next day the members of the NGO picked Rahul up from his hotel. The route from Mawa Ghat to Bagerhat was shorter but they went via Aricha as they had some work in Manikganj.

Their car crossed Manikganj and went on ahead. Their destination was Kaliganga river and the village called Andharmanik beyond it. They left the car on the bank of the river, used a small boat to cross it and reached Andharmanik. Rahul was with his team. Bhaktadas Mandal's house was close to where they got off the boat. Earlier he used to be a court clerk, now he collected toll tax here on a daily wage of eighty rupees. His house, on a large plot of nineteen *Bighas,* was at a little distance and adjoining it was an orchard of banana trees spread over thirty *Bighas.* His wife, son Subrata and daughter Suchita were on their own at home. Though they somehow lived in the house during the day, they dared not do it at night. They generally hid themselves somewhere at night, scared of being attacked by militants. They did not know where Bhaktadas was. Parveen, who was part of the team, had been posted in this district for three years and knew it in and out. She walked a little distance and entered a house. Only Rahul was with her, the others were at Bhaktadas' house. The owner of the house which they had entered, was taken aback by them. Parveen handed him a piece of paper and told him to read what was written on it. "Then I will talk to you." The note was from his son who lived in the Jagannath Hall in Dhaka University. He went for tuition to Parveen's sister five days a week. Parveen had heard about Bhaktadas from him. When the owner of the house had read the letter, he took them inside and shortly a scared looking Bhaktadas appeared before them. Parveen put him at ease. "There is nothing to fear. Tell us in detail about what happened to you."

Bhaktadas: "What can I say?" He started sobbing.

Parveen: "This time you worked for BNP, didn't you?"

Bhaktadas: "Yes."

Parveen: "Then why are you being singled out for attack?"

Bhaktadas: "That I do not know. But I have heard that the market near our house will be extended. So they need the land on which my house is built."

Parveen: "Who are 'they'?"

Bhaktadas: "Badal, Parvez and others."

Parveen: "Are they from BNP?"

Bhaktadas: "Yes, Badal is the leader of the youth wing and Parvez of the students' wing."

Parveen: "Did they put a pistol on your temple on the river bank?"

Bhaktadas: "There were three others with them. Badal

threatened me at gunpoint and said that unless I gave him fifty thousand rupees by the next day I would have to leave my house."

Rahul: "You just told us that you worked for them and voted for them. Then why are they asking you for money?"

Bhaktadas: "What a thing to say! I cannot tell you anything. Maybe they are behaving in this manner with me because I am a Hindu. I paid them three thousand rupees. I also told them that I would give them some more after I sold bananas, but they were not willing to wait. They said that they would kidnap my daughter if I did not pay up. My daughter was so scared that she stopped going to school. You can see that I am also on the run."

Rahul: "How old is your daughter?"

Bhaktadas: "Sixteen."

Saying this he fell at Rahul's feet and started crying. "Save me and my family. I cannot leave my house and go away. How can I leave my ancestral house where my parents and grandparents lived all thei lives? Please save us."

Rahul had not revealed his true identity. He had let it be known that he had come with Parveen. He tried to console Bhaktadas, putting his arms round the hapless man. Bhaktadas sobbed louder. Parveen said, "We are aware of your plight. That is why we have come to talk to you. If you cry so loudly someone will hear you. Here, take this. Our NGO has collected ten thousand rupees for you. But please spend it on your family. Don't give it away to the extortionists."

It was late afternoon by the time Rahul reached Bagerhat with the members of the NGO. They were scheduled to stay here for four more days. On the first day they made a survey of the

Rampal and Mangala areas. Bagerhat was close to the Sundérbans and there were a number of fish farms and prawn farms here. Most of the farms dealt in Bagda prawns which thrived in salt water. In the eighties, the affluent persons in the region had encroached upon land belonging to others and set up prawn farms. The landowners were not able to stop them from landgrabbing. Those who tried were eliminated. Many people lost their land and lives during this time. Till early ninety six, the trade in prawn thrived in this manner. During the ninety six elections when the Awami League came into power many of these illegally built prawn farms were razed. Those in power earlier had to lose the land and prawn farms which had been such profitable ventures for them. The land went back to the lawful owners. Around this time Nikhil, Jiten and others of Nalbuniya village in the Kathmari Union got back land which had been taken from them earlier. They had invested all that they had on

the land and put up prawn farms and the venture proved to be a profitable one. But trouble loomed large the day after the eighth General Elections. Attacks were made on their farms in an attempt to recapture them and there were large scale thefts and robberies. Their houses were not spared either. There were around a hundred Hindu families in the Shaguna village in the Winetala Union. Every house was attacked along with the farms. Most of the Hindu families in this region suffered the same fate. In Bakultala village itself, ninety prawn farms were grabbed. None of the Hindus in the area were spared. Even poor fishermen were deprived of the small ponds from which they eked out a living.

Chittaranjan Mandal had been admitted in the Rampal Health Centre. He had been sleeping in his small prawn farm as usual. Militants attacked his farm beat him up, looted it and left him taking him for dead. Rahul asked Chittaranjan, a teacher by profession, "Did you recognize the people who attacked you?"

Chittaranjan: "I am lucky to be alive. I don't want to lose my family by opening my mouth."

His wife, sitting by his bedside, in the hospital, said, "If there is life, there is hope. Let them take what they want."

Rahul: "Who are these people?"

"Those who have won the elections. Members of the BNP and the Jamat-e-Islam. These are the people who are looting others. Why don't you find out for yourselves."

"Who injured you so badly?" Rahul asked.

"Could not recognize them in the darkness. But I know who is behind these attacks. It is Fakir Taiyeb-ur-Rehman."

Eight

Rahul came to a village called Utkul. The Hindus in this village lived in the Sahapara and Daspara areas. As soon as Rahul entered the village with members of the NGO, a few young men started trailing them. Some of these men had beards and others had caps on. They were dressed in kurta pyjama and white sports shoes which appeared inexpensive. After following them for some time, these young men turned back and another group took their place. They were dressed differently – in shirts and trousers or trousers with Tshirts. None of them had beards or wore caps. Parveen whispered to Rahul that the first group consisted of members of the Jamat-e-Islam whereas the second one was made up of workers of the Bangladesh Nationalist Party or the BNP. They generally sat in groups in villages and followed newcomers to keep an eye on them. If the visitors were in a small group, they were interrogated and then allowed to pass.

However No one asked them any thing. Rahul wanted to talk to them about the picture of General Zia-ur-Rehman and the ear of grain on their caps. But Parveen told him not to. Talking to them would only encourage them to misbehave. When the team entered Sahapara, the boys went back to where they had been hanging out earlier. Their job had been to find out where they were going, something that they would report to 'big brother'. Now they were certain that the visitors were going to the homes of Hindus, there was no need to follow them any further. Even Parveen did not know why they did not follow them further. She had done her homework and found out quite a few things from different sources. But she had not been able to find out anything about these persons.

All activities seemed to have come to a stop in Utkul. In Sahapara and Daspara one could not see a girl or woman anywhere as they had all been sent to safer places the day before the elections as soon as their guardians had sensed trouble. The people here were very scared and not ready to talk. Despite sustained efforts nothing could be got out of them. When people were asked where the young men and boys were, they were evasive. Finally when the team was returning, Rahul saw a woman with a long veil covering her face, washing some green vegetables, he desperately wanted to talk to her. But she did not respond to any of his questions. Rahul asked Parveen why no one was ready to talk to them. She said that the people who had followed them earlier would go to the houses in the village which the team had visited and want to know what had gone on. If not provided satisfying answers, they would threaten them, even beat them. That is why the villagers had decided not to open their mouths.

Villages like Kartikdiya, Matrapur, Kodamara, Chaparkul and others were located on both sides of the Chitra river. These villages had a lush green, peaceful appearance. The small huts looked like cosy little nests. Altogether, the sight of these villages in sylvan setting made one happy. They seemed so natural, whereas even the greenery in cities appeared unnatural and one was choked by pollution and likely to fall ill. One could bathe in moonlight in any part of the village and soak it up on a Purnima night. That was not possible in a city. In Dhaka one could not see the moon so clearly, let alone soak up its light.

Workers and supporters of the four party coalition had blacklisted all the Hindus in these beautiful looking villages on the day following the elections. They were singling them out. Narayan Mridha of Kuliadaid village was one of them. They had beaten him up. The headmaster of Kakharpur Collegiate School had suffered the same fate. Most of those who had stabbed the schoolmaster had ben his students. His only crime was that he was a Hindu and had voted for the Awami League. This was something that they took for granted. All Hindus voted for the Awami League. So they should be finished off or tortured so that they left the country. That was the only way to defeat the Awami League. This decision was not that of workers at the village level, it must have been taken by senior party executives, thought Rahul. That is why Hindus were being exploited in a very systematic manner. Rahul now realized why atrocities on Hindus were being committed more in villages as compared to towns.

The people in these villages had not kept their mouths shut like those in Utkul. So Persons like Nilay Kumar, Arun Kumar,

Alok Kumar and others had been beaten up very badly with iron rods and hammers. They could not even get medical help for their injuries as the militants had threatened the doctors. So complications had set in. Alok Kumar's foot had become gangrenous. Narayan Das, an elderly person in Koshmara, had just married off his only son Gopal three months back. But two days after the elections, a group of twenty intruders barged into his house, beat up Gopal very badly and gangraped his new bride Bijli. When Narayan Das tried to intervene, he was pushed aside so hard that he fell on a boulder, broke six teeth and fell down unconscious.

Rahul started writing his report after visiting Bahul, another Hindu village in the Chitalmari with Parveen.He had sent daily reports after coming to Bagerhat. Email facilities were not available here; he would have to send a fax today. All kinds of atrocities like rape, arson, looting had been committed in these villages for six days after the elections. That was followed by extortion. Hindus were told that they would have to pay up if they wanted to live here for the next five years. If they did not pay up their women would have to pay with their honour. If even that was not possible, they should be ready to give up their properties and migrate to the other side of the border. The local office bearers of the four party coalition had noted down names of all the Hindu families in their areas. Even the sum of money to be given had been fixed up – five thousand for a poor family and ten thousand for the slightly more affluent. In certain cases, this sum could be raised to fifty thousand or even a lakh as the case might be. Those who could not pay up, ran away, leaving their ancestral homes, in the cover of darkness. No one knew where they had gone. One wondered whether they had crossed over and gone to West Bengal.

The Hindu shopkeepers were not spared either. Those who paid up were allowed to open their shops, others who were unable to pay had to close down. They were not allowed to open their shops. Many shops were looted and damaged because the owners had not paid up. Since Nepal of Bansbedia was not able to pay, eighteen Taka, all that he had, were snatched from him. Dr jagadish Halder of Santoshpur was asked to pay one lakh Taka. Asimanand, Arnab and Horen of Dumuria were asked to pay fifty thousand Taka each. They were also told when to pay the money. Rahul came to know that this practice was rampant not only in Bagerhat but in other districts as well. The number of Hindus in Bagerhat was a little over three lakhs. Even before the elections, they were busy making plans for the Durga Puja. But extortions and the atrocities dampened their enthusiasm for the Puja celebrations. They had nothing to celebrate now. Nothing to do except sigh and mourn their fate.

Temples and images were not spared by the supporters and office bearers of the four party coalition. They had damaged images of Durga and driven away the artisans making them, after beating them up. Members of Hindu families in this district had been separated from each other. What occasion did they have to celebrate, a person asked Rahul.

The Puja Shubarambh Committee in Dhaka had decided that this time Durga Puja would be celebrated in an austre manner. But what about the decorations? Was it possible to conduct the Puja without them? But what about the circumstances, Manoranjan Das of Khaserhat asked Rahul. The latter had no answer. His work was to convey the questions to his readers and let them look for answers. That he was doing. The Government had announced that it would give financial aid to Hindus so that they could carry on with Puja celebrations. Rahul had reported that as well. He wondered how the Government was going to do it when there were just three days left for the Puja to start.

He concluded, "The police as well as the militants were putting pressure on the people to put up a show of normalcy. 'How can we live under so much pressure? We don't know how long we will have to live in under such conditions. We don't want anything except peace.' Achintya Debnath's wife seemed to echo the feelings of all the Hindus."

From Bagerhat Rahul went along with the team to Pirojpur. They were supposed to spend a day here. They were proceeding according to the plans made by Parveen. She had done the homework on the areas which the team was supposed to visit. Now she was guiding the team. If Rahul had not come with them, he would never have been able to visit the interiors and gather information, he reminded himself.

As they visited Pirojpur and Nadirpur, they met Dr Deblal Dakua.He was the most popular doctor in the entire area. But he did not earn much money. How could he? He did not take any money from the poor, not even for the medicines he gave them. He did not care what their community or religion was. He considered it a crime to take money from the poor. As a result he had never been able to save any money though they were not starving either.

One evening Dr Deblal was going to examine a patient in

south Baniari village. When he passed the tea shop of Hannan Fakir, some young men called him and surrounded him. He knew these boys and had often seen them here. They had come to his clinic to ask him to vote for the BNP.

First they humiliated him and then one of them shouted to the others to get a blade so that this *Malaun*(a derogatory term used for Hindus) could be circumscribed and taught a lesson. "Let me make this son of a pig a Muslim." Dr Deblal got scared at this kind of behaviour from boys who were young enough to be his sons. He could not stifle a scream when they really got a blade and started taking off his clothes. But no one came to help him despite his screams. A large crowd watched from a distance but no one uttered a single word, let alone help. A man called Liyakat made lewd gestures at him. Deblal asked him for water but the boys wanted to piss into his mouth. One of them even brought a bowl full of urine and forced him to drink it. The poor doctor could do nothing to stop them.

After that the boys changed their original plan of circumscribing him. One of them, who seemed to be the leader of the group, told him sternly, "We can leave you but on one condition. Within a week you will have to pay up fifty thousand Taka. If you don't, you can say goodbye to life." They threatened him that his son who worked with the police, would be dismissed if he did not do what they said. They also threatened to rape his wife and daughter. He was made to sign on a blank paper. From that day he had been threatened many times and his wife abused. Deblal told Rahul and his team that he could not afford to pay up fifty thousand Taka and told the police about it. He had even lodged a report at the Nazirpur police station but to no avail. As he spoke about the threat to his wife and daughter, Deblal broke down and said that it was not possible for them to live there any more.

Rahul and his team stopped at Gopalganj that day. Durga Puja had started but Rahul did not notice any place where it was being celebrated. On the next day, they visited a place called Ramsheel. On the way they stopped and spoke to Shefali Halder, elected member from Bajihar Union Council of Barisal. She started sobbing loudly as she spoke of the atrocities inflicted on her by militants belonging to the four party alliance.

At Ramsheel they came across a number of men and women who had suffered in many ways. Parveen had to cover her tearful face with her handkerchief when she saw the ravaged and expressionless face of a young woman who was nine months pregnant. There were so many heartrending incidents, mother and daughter being raped in front of each other, daughter in law and mother in law suffering criminal assault in the hands of the same person.It was an unending list of grievances that the team had to listen to. Instances of women being stripped and subjected to all kinds of sexual perversions when the men were not to be found. These poor people had tried all kinds of desperate things to save their lives and honour, like trying to escape in a boat under cover of darkness, swimming across a deep nullah, it was a long list. But nothing had helped. A middle aged working woman called Sadhana Debi said that some young men barged into her house on the pretext of asking her to give them nine thousand Taka. Then these boys, young enough to be her sons, raped her one by one, at knifepoint. The same group had approached her before the elections asking her to vote for the

BNP. She did go to vote but was told that her vote had already been cast. Another instance was that of some young boys breaking into a house where a woman was sleeping with her daughter. They raped both mother and daughter and left with the threat that if they dared to tell anyone, they would be killed. All these persons who had suffered , had just one question, "Is it a crime to be a Hindu?" Rahul had no answer to this, neither did Parveen.It was not possible to answer such a question.

The same night they came back to Dhaka. When Rahul reached his hotel, he was told that there had been three calls for him. All three had been from his editor. This time he had not been able to leave any contact number for him. He rang up and told his editor about his return. When his editor told him to do a story on Durga Puja celebrations. Rahul said that no one except Bengalis would be interested in it. The editor was irritated and told Rahul that he was asking him to do a story for that very reason. "All right." Rahul said and kept the phone down.

The next day Rahul started for the Ramakrishna Mission after breakfast. This was the day of Kumari Puja but Rahul was disappointed to see only a small group of persons. As he turned the corner near the south of Motijheel the police stopped his auto. He could not go up to the gate in an auto. Rahul decided to walk, it was only a small distance. After a while he stopped. He had noticed something odd. There were more policemen than persons who had come to see the Puja. He asked himself, "Is the Puja being conducted by the police?" Rahul asked a person,

"What is your name?"

"A.K.Mukharjee."

"Have you come here for the first time today?"

"No, I have been coming here for the last thirty years."

"Do you notice any change this year?"

"Last year the Hindus had celebrated the Puja with great enthusiasm and joy. This year it seems that the Government is conducting the Puja."

"Are the Hindus conducting the Puja under pressure?"

"Isn't that obvious?"

"Why? Don't they want to do Puja this year?"

"After all that has happened, does anyone feel like celebrating anything?"

"Are there always such crowds on the day of the Kumari Puja?"

"This is nothing. Earlier I could not have stood in one place and talked to you as I am doing today. We would have been separated by the crowd much earlier. Can you see those unoccupied chairs? In the last thirty years that I have been coming here, I have been able to find a seat for myself only two or three times."

"Is the situation the same throughout the country?"

"Absolutely."

Rahul did not ask him anything else. He walked on ahead.

He walked out of the Ramakrishna Mission, visited a few more pandals and returned to the hotel. He wanted to talk to a few more persons before sending his story. He thought he would look through the newspapers in Dhaka to see how they had covered the Puja. He rang up some people and talked to them about this. Then he set out for the office of *Bhorer Kagaj* . Here security was not as stringent as that in *Jankanth.* He went up to the fourth floor without being stopped. He knew the editor

Benazir Ahmed. He talked to him for some time and then asked for the files of newspapers and magazines. Benazir Ahmed had them brought out for him and Rahul glanced through the news coverage of the Durga Puja. Then he went out to a cyber café.

He started writing his story. Though Durga is known as *anandamayi* – one whose arrival brings joy to all her worshippers, this time it is being celebrated mechanically, without any enthusiasm. There was not the slightest trace of joy anywhere, it was a festival only in name. There were more policemen in the Puja pandals, than devotees. Even those present looked anything but happy. Most of those present seemed overwhelmed by grief and anxiety. In the districts around Dhaka, the persons who had been earlier involved in acts of violence, arson, looting and gang rapes had a special role to play during the Puja. They were the ones who had forced the Hindus to take part in the Puja despite their grief and anger. Most of these Hindus who had suffered immeasurably, were still homeless. But the idea was to show that everything was normal, nothing untoward had happened. The newly elected Government was determined to publicize the fact that 'nothing had happened'. In some places like Khulna, Barisal, Bagerhat and others, those associated with the ruling party had collected subscription themselves and were conducting the Puja themselves. In some areas, large sums of money had been distributed to proclaim to the world that the Puja was being celebrated in a grand manner. This time there were no fancy decorations or illumination, not even mikes, nor the cultural programmes that one associated with the Puja. The Puja had to be conducted and it was. There was nothing festive about it.

Nine

On the day of Navami, fifteen diplomats from different embassies and diplomatic missions in Dhaka were taken around thirty Puja pandals selected from sixteen districts. These diplomats were taken by helicopters, accompanied by ministers.

The purpose was to get these diplomats to certify that the Puja was being celebrated as usual. The only purpose of the Government was to keep up its image and a facade of secularism. However, all this could not hide the real state of things.

In Chittagong, the organizers of one hundred and sixty three Puja committees were planning to protest against the way in which Hindus were being victimized. They were planning a hunger strike from dawn to dusk. On the day of Navami they were planning to form a human chain and maintain a silence for one hour. Apart from this there were no lights or mikes in he pandals, only black flags as a mark of protest.

In Khulna, there were thirty Pujas in the two thousand five hundred and twenty four districts, half as compared to the previous year. In most places they had been organized because of administrative and political pressure. Naturally the spirit of joy, the festive mood was totally missing.

Rahul completed his report and pressed the button marked 'send'.

The next day when Rahul read the *Daily Star,* he got a shock. Till now this well known newspaper had chosen to blank out news about the atrocities on Hindus altogether. In fact even the press conference of Purnima Seal had been reported very briefly. But today the weekly supplement had a cover story titled 'A Puja Marred'. The story which ran to ten pages, was titled; 'A Festival Spoiled by Violence'. If the diplomats who had said the previous day that things were normal in the country were to see this, what would their reaction be. Would they not feel guilty?

Rahul had a stomach infection within three days of returning to Dhaka. Ultiately he had to go to a doctor. He met Dr. Suman Lahiri who invited him over to lunch. Rahul had promised to go. Suman had said that he would pick him up from the hotel at one as it was a holiday for him. Bijayadashami was a holiday but this time it fell on a Friday, which was the doctor's weekly off. He told Rahul that he had also invited a few others. Among them was Nirmalendu Goon, a well known poet who had been stunned by the carnage to the extent he did not even want to talk about it. So, he had chosen another topic to discuss – US attack on Afganistan to catch Osama bin Laden. He went on talking on this but stopped suddenly when Mihir, a student leader entered the room. Mihir had met Rahul earlier. He had come to his hotel with Suman who had introduced him as a friend and member of his organization.

"What organization is this?"

"We have formed an association of homosexuals and lesbians."

"How many members are there?"

"Over a hundred."

"Are there other such organizations in this country?"

"No."

"Are any of your members married?"

"No, none of them are married."

"Is your organization recognized by the government?"

"We are a registered body. But the name under we are registered does not mention homosexuality or lesbianism."

"If it had been mentioned, you would not have managed to get registered. Isn't it?"

"No, absolutely not."

"Do you know how many persons like you are there in this country?"

"I won't be able to give you the exact figure."

"What about Dhaka?"

"That also I am not sure about."

"That is because they have not come out in the open. But we think that there are large numbers of such persons in hostels for young girls and boys. More than those in hostels attached to Madarasas."

"Oh, is that so?"

"Yes."

An image of Durga was being taken to the river Buriganga for immersion. There were large numbers of policemen and jawans of Bangladesh Rifles. They came on to the verandah to see. Nirmalendu Goon folded his hands as a mark of respect to the image. He said, "This is the first time I am setting my eyes on the goddess Durga this year."

Rahul wanted to know if the heavy police and army bandobast was a regular feature.

The poet Goon said, "No, no. This is the first time I have seen it."

Rahul did not ask any more questions. People like Nirmalendu Goon who had been so involved with Puja had not even gone to the pandal this year. They were obviously deeply hurt. Rahul did not to hurt them any more.

As they were having their lunch, Mihir took out a sheet of paper from his pocket and gave it to the poet. He read it, put it on the table and said nothing. Rahul asked him if he could read it. It was a photocopy and said,"Brother Hindus, do not conduct the Puja this year. The images of Durga have been shattered. Tell your chairman to go to India and take you with them. If you persist, there will be bomb explosions in the pandals." Rahul kept the sheet in his pocket after reading it. Mihir told him to keep it. He talked to Rahul for about an hour after lunch. This would be the base of today's story. He had the slip of paper. That was evidence to substantiate his story.

Rahul sat in the cyber café and started writing. "After the elections, the Durga Puja was conducted under heavy police protection even as Hindus were subjected to all kinds of tortures and attacks. Today was the last day of the Puja and one could feel the grimness. After the immersion there were shows of protest in every temple and Puja pandal. The images were immersed in the Buriganga under heavy police protection."Rahul stopped for a while. Then he continues, "There are news of images being broken and arson in the Puja pandals all over the country. In Nowgaon a pandal had been torched. In Kulaura in the Sylhet district an image had been broken. In Sarsandi, temples as well as the image of Durga had been broken and at least ten houses of Hindus had been attacked and robbed in one night. Ten persons had been robbed and injured in attacks on Hindu houses in Natore. The marauders did not spare even a blind person in Tillagram in the Kaligram district of Jhinaidah.In a sub division of Pirojpur, the genitals of Nirmal Halder, a teacher, were cut off by his students. It was a horrifying story everywhere. Touts were earning a fat commission by ferrying Hindus across the border at the Hilli port. News of rape, attacks on Hindus, arson, plunder were commonplace. After writing all this, Rahul took out the piece of paper given by Mihir and quoted it after translating it into English. In the last paragraph he referred to the itinerary of the special emissary sent by the Government of India to Dhaka. Earlier, the Bangladesh High Commission in Delhi had been asked by the Ministry of External Affairs to give a correct picture of the atrocities as there had been demonstrations in front of the Commission. Rahul then sent off his story. Suddenly he realized that he had not mentioned anything about the torture cell at Jagannath Hall, the only hostel for minorities at the Dhaka University with the connivance of Nasiruddin Pintoo, a BNP MP.

Rahul came back to the hotel. Just as he was about to go to

the rest room, the phone rang. It was his editor. He told Rahul to find out if the talks between Brajesh Mishra, Defence Adirsos Government of India , the Bangladesh Government, the opposition and members of Hindu organizations or Hindu leaders took up the atrocities on Hindus. He was to find out and report it.

Rahul felt like talking to his wife. It was eight in Dhaka, it would be seven thirty in Delhi. He did not want to wake her up at such an early hour, but the urge was great and he rang up. He had spoken to her the day before yesterday and she said that his daughter was missing him. It was a way of conveying to him how much he was being missed. He was also missing them a lot, but did not want to talk about it. She spoke to him, still half asleep. Then he went down for breakfast. Today he was supposed to go to Kaliakoir, quite far from Dhaka. He had to find out about the meeting with Brajesh Mishra. Could both the things be done on the same day, he asked himself.

Kaliakoir was on the banks of the river Banshi. It was an important business centre. Most of the businessmen here were Hindus. When Rahul reached there he noticed that most of the shops were closed as people had moved away in search of safer places. They had been threatened that they would be sent away to India if they did not pay up. Hilaluddin Ahmed was the leader of the extortionists. The shops of the Hindus who had left had been forcibly occupied by his men who had put their own locks on them. The secretary of the local press club said that it did not seem that those who had gone away would ever come back. Even if they did they would have to pay up before they could open their shops or pay with their lives.

On returning to Dhaka Rahul did not go to his hotel. Brajesh Mishra had already met the newly elected leaders of the opposition and the Prime Minister. They had talked about the atrocities on Hindus, security measures to be taken to prevent such incidents in future, drilling of natural gas as per agenda, after which he had gone back to India. The Prime Minister had assured him that he would personally oversee safety measures for Hindus. A four member delegation from the progressive and enlightened section of society was supposed to meet him in his suite. They did not come at the designated time. A man who said he represented them had come instead to get the appointment cancelled. Rahul came to know this from Brajesh Mishra's Officer-in-appointing. Rahul tried to find out the reason.Rahul had got the information that the government had prepared a list of individuals and organizations who represented minorities. Was the delegation scheduled to meet Brajesh Mishra not included in the list? Nothing could be said for cetain, Rahul could only hazaed a guess. Only those who were supposed to come, could give him the correct answer. Rahul spoke to one of them and sent off his story. Today he sent two stories, one on Kaliakoir, the other on Brajesh Mishra's visit.

The organization called Udichi had a significant role to play in the progressive movement in the country. Today Udichi was celebrating its founder's day. Inaugurating the celebrations, Wahidul Haq, known to be a great supporter of progressive thinking and non-communal awareness, said in his speech, "It has been established that except for two crore and sixty lakhs out of a total population of thirteen crores, everyone was a coward. Political and cultural battles had to be waged against those who had dared to taint the identity of the Bengali. Purnimarani Seal of Sirajganj would be the mascot of the struggfle.we have to keep her photograph in every house and take an oath before it to fight injustice and discrimination." Rahul clarified in the story he sent,"The four party coalition has received two crore sixty lakh votes. It was decided that Wahidul Haq would go to Purnima's house in Sirajganj on behalf of all organizations and communities, to ask for forgiveness. The fact that there were people like Wahidul Haq in Bangladesh, made it possible for people from non-Muslims to stay here. Sadly though, the number of such persons was dwindling.

Rahul had visited an extension of Dhaka called Uttara where the International Institute for the Mother Tongue used to be, on house number 19, 15th street sector 3 Rabindra Sarani. But it was not there any more. There was a big lock on the main gate. On 21 February 1952 the demonstrations to promote their mother tongue put Bengalis on the world map. But the movement had not received any international recognition for about fifty years. Ultimately on 17 November 2000 the United Nations gave recognition to the language movement and declared 21 February as the International Day for the Mother tongue. The Awami League

Government had set up the International Mother Tongue Institute. The purpose was to bring together all languages of the world, put them in their context and nurture them so that they did not become extinct. Efforts were made through the internet to bring together all languages of the world, open websites, revive languages which had been lost in the march of progress, put them in their context and help the government to study and research various languages.

But after the elections the new Government was bent on closing this institute, Rahul did not understand why. It could not be just because it had been set up by the Awami Government. The Hindus employed by the Awami League Government at every level, had either been dismissed or demoted. During the Awami tenure a Hindu could get to the position of a secretary in the Government. Since the Partition in 1947 no one had been so liberal and fair with the Hindus. Of course this did not mean that the Government had given out of turn promotions to Hindus. It was just that they had not interfered with their ACR like other governments, just allowed a free and fair system to evolve. The Government had also tried to put an end to communalism but it failed in that. That is why fundamentalist forces had taken over the entire country today. Why had the Awami government failed, Rahul asked himself. Was it because some people were hellbent on keeping communalism alive? Maybe.

After being defeated badly, Sheikh Hasina had sent teams of former leaders of student unions to different parts of the country so that reasons for the defeat could be found out. The teams had been asked to prepare reports. For a fortnight, the twenty five member team went all over the country in different groups. They spoke to people from different social levels. Their reports indicated that the four hundred and fifty polling booths in the country were in a way captured by the BNP goons. In one hundred and fifty seats Awami candidates were defeated by force. Thirty seats were lost in inner party fights. The vendetta and lawlessness that followed in the wake of the elections was responsible for the death of at least a hundred persons. Around ten thousand persons had been injured. Another ten thousand persons had been hounded out of their homes by threats of extortion and concocted lawsuits. More than a lakh houses and business organizations had suffered because of arson and looting. The list of those afflicted showed mostly Hindu names, along with a few names of supporters, workers and leaders of the Awami League.

While returning from Uttara Rahul took a round of Shyamali. Twenty year old Narayan Chandra Ghosh from the village Adani in Rajshahi district was fighting death. Eight militants had attacked Ghoshpara, where he lived in the darkness of midnight. These were the same people who had come earlier, asking them to vote for the BNP. They broke into Shiprarani Ghosh's house. Shiprarani and her seventeen year old daughter Rekha were inside. When they tried to abduct Rekha she clung to her mother in fear. Poor Shipra fell at the feet of the leader of the gang and begged him not to rape her daughter, that would kill her. They could molest her, she had said. As she sat on the hospital bed next to her brother Narayan, she talked about the incident. Her brother, also from the same village, had tried to run away as soon as his house was attacked. But he had tripped and fallen in front of the Darpana theatre and the attackers had caught up with him. The militants from Jamat-e-Islam had cut the veins of his feet.

Ten

Allegations of atrocities on minorities and the fact that they were fleeing the country, were to be investigated by a commission appointed by the cabinet. This was to be headed by the Chief Secretary of the Prime Minister. The commission was told to prepare its report within a week. It had been decided to conduct an investigation on four levels, involving ministers, MPs, secretaries and diplomats. Ministers had been told to survey the affected areas and tabulate the results. The regions including border districts from where reports of atrocities on minorities and large scale border crossing had come in, were to be surveyed by MPs who were then to present their reports like the ministers. The Bangladesh Deputy High Commission in Kolkata had been entrusted with the task of finding out whether the reports of minorities crossing over into India were true, by going to the said areas and seeing for itself.

Rahul stopped writing. Wouldn't it be better to talk to a few more people? His story would sound more authentic if could get to know what people thought of the commission. He switched off the computer and went out after ringing up some persons. The Vice Chancellor of National University lived on road no. 11 in Dhanmandi. His name was Professor Durgadas Bhattacharjee. During the tenure of the caretaker government, Professor Bhattacharjee had been removed from his post and another man with the right kind of connections appointed in his place. His greatest qualification was that he was a Muslim. After the partition of the country Professor Bhattacharjee was the first Hindu to become a Vice Chancellor in this country. Even after being removed from his post, he had not vacated his official residence. He could retain it for six months according to the rules. Where would he go from here? He did not have a house in Dhaka. He had not been worldly enough to buy a house in Dhaka while working at the university. He was thinking of going back to his old position in the Dhaka University so that he could be allotted residential quarters. He would move into that, he had thought.

As he rang the bell, the guard asked from inside whom he wanted to meet. When he took the name of Durgadas Bhattacharjee, the gate was opened and he was ushered in. Dr Bhattacharjee came down, and greeted Rahul as he offered his card. As he sat down he asked if Rahul would like some tea. Rahul said yes and wanted to know his opinion about the enquiry commission.

"See, the commission has been asked to file in its report within a week. Tell me, is it possible to complete a report of something that has taken place on such a large scale, in such a short time?"

"Why not?" Rahul had a counter question.

"I am sure you are aware that about forty lakh Hindus have been victimised right from the days of the caretaker government to the present when the four party coalition has assumed power. Numerous temples have been razed and images disfigured. Total damages would run to thousands of crores. Of course money is not the only yardstick to measure such damages..."

Durgadas Bhattacharjee stopped suddenly and lowered his eyes.

Rahul sensed his agony and said sorry.

"No,no, it is all right. I was going to say that about a thousand women have been raped. This cannot be measured in terms of money. Besides, thirty thousand Hindus have been driven out of their ancestral houses. Who is going to look for them? Is it possible to prepare a report of such scale carnage in just one week?"

"Maybe they will extend the time if the report is not ready within a week."

"The time factor is not all that important. What matters is sincerity, sympathy...."

"If that had not been there, why was the commission set up, in the first place?"

"Must have been under some kind of pressure." Bhattacharjee said.

"But the government has been constantly denying the fact that minorities have been victimised. Hasn't it proved itself a liar by setting up the commission?"

"Yes, of course. It was just an eyewash for those at home and abroad. The government was compelled to set up the commission but it is least bothered about the inquiry."

"This means that you have no faith in the findings of the commission."

"I can tell you right now what the report is going to be. It will say that no houses have been occupied by force. It will concede that there have been a few untoward incidents for which the local Awami leaders and workers are to be blamed. The Deputy High Commission in Kolkata will testify that no Bangladeshi citizen had crossed over to India."

Rahul came out of Bhattacharjee's house and walked down to Dhaka University. The British Council was some way off from the Vice Chancellor's residence. Rahul walked in the opposite direction towards the quarters for teachers. He did not have much difficulty in locating the flat of Professor Abu Hasnat. He introduced himself to Prof. Hasnat and wanted his views on the inquiry commission.

"I have heard that during his visit to US the Foreign Minister was questioned on atrocities on minorities by two members of the American Congress. Apart from this, the European Union has taken a stand against the oppression of the minorities. It has appealed to the human rights organizations to stop work in the region. Mary Robinson, the chief of UNHCHR has held meetings with lawyers and the media on this issue. I feel that the Government was compelled to institute an Enquiry Commission, because of these reasons despite constant denials about atrocities on minorities.

Professor Hasnat went and got a few newspapers. He gave them to Rahul and said, "The newspapers have been reporting atrocities on minorities practically every day. I can't understand how the Government can persist with its denials."

Rahul glanced the newspapers-old and recent. 'Panic in Dumuria: they have told us to go to India, old Kanchan Dasi says'. A news item from Hajiganj and Shahrast in Chandpur 'The Awami League threatens minorities with dire consequences if they vote'. 'In Daspara village in Mirsarai of Chittagong district, a priest murdered, thirty dead after attack by BNP henchmen' A man who grew a beard and voted for the Awami League has his beard pulled out'. Rahul had most of this earlier. He asked, "What do you expect from the Enquiry Commission?"

Hasnat said, "It is not what I expect that is important. I want the enquiry to be impartial so that the truth comes out. But, from earlier experiences I am apprehensive, even pessimistic about the outcome. After our *Muktiyuddha*(freedom struggle) the country has not witnessed such large scale violence, attacks and oppression before. In the last thirty years whenever atrocities were committed on minorities and enquiries conducted, no report came out with the truth. This time the repression appeared rather planned. Jamat-e-Islam is one of the parties in the Four Party Alliance. What they could not complete in 1971, they are now doing officially, as using their official strength. The repression on minorities is still continuing, it is not incidental, but a rather well orchestrated and planned one. Do you think the Commission will admit it?"

"I only want to know your opinion on the matter." Rahul said.

The Enquiry Commission has been set up to hide the truth, not reveal it. We are trying to do something about it with the help of progressive and conscientious persons in the country. We will take help from NGOs in this matter. We want to expose the true picture of the oppression through an impartial enquiry."

Rahul came back to the cyber café in the Isa Khan Complex. He opened his file and started writing again. He completed his story and read what he had written. He checked two spellings about which he was not sure and sent the story to his editor.

Rahul went to Feni, three hours journey from Dhaka. He had been here earlier when Sheikh Hasina was here as part of a campaigning tour of the country. Rahul had come a few days earlier, to cover the eighth General Elections in Bangladesh.He had come to Feni with Jamal who was covering Sheikh Hasina's Feni Visit. This time he did not need anyone. Earlier he did not manage to visit the place properly something that he wanted to do this time. Feni shared a border with Tripura and if the partition had been geographical, it would have been a part of India and Rahul could have visited it without passport or visa. The thought made him happy. Suddenly, as he remembered his visit to Bhola and his father's words, his mood changed. His father had been compelled to leave his birthplace, ancestral home, land and all that was dear to him because of the political boundaries. The repression on Hindus that had started with the Partition was still continuing. He did not know when it would stop. Maybe when all the Hindus had been killed or crossed over to India. Was this being done to drive the Hindus away from Bangladesh as had been done in Pakistan? Rahul wondered how many Hindus were left in Pakistan. Did Pakistan attain peace by driving Hindus away? Now the Muslims were fighting amongst themselves. Would the same thing happen in Bangladesh once all the Hindus had been killed or driven away? Maybe this country would have the same fate as Pakistan. That would not surprise Rahul.

The Awami League Government had constantly tried to establish Bangladesh as a secular state and strengthen the foundations of democracy so that it became institutional within the country. But it did not seem that it could still persist with its effort. The party formed by General Zia with the help of some Maoists and Pakistan loyalists was in power now. The party formed took its guidelines from these countries. Of these, Pakistan had no democracy even after half a century of independence. Any effort to revive democracy there was crushed by the army. And in China, those who demand democracy are promptly shot down. The efforts made by the earlier regime to establish democracy in this country were sure to die out for want of care. As these thoughts nagged Rahul, he tried to get them out of his head and walked towards Sonapur village outside the town of Feni. He planned to visit Satbaria, Safarpur and Motiganj after that. A bus stopped and a woman got on to it. Rahul heard two boys sitting on the front seat, asking her in a taunting manner, "So, didi you are still here!" she did not answer, just stood quietly. Rahul looked at her carefully. She was about twenty five or thirty years old and appeared to be a married Hindu woman from the *sindur* in her parting and the white and red bangles on her wrists. She carried a sling bag and clutched a file in her hands. Rahul was not curious about the contents of the file. He wanted to know what the boys were hinting at.

The two boys again said in a loud voice, "Let didi sit down." Rahul could not make head or tail of what thy meant. Should he ask them? No, that would not be proper, though he was getting more and more curious. He asked the boys casually what they wanted to say. The two boys laughed loudly and said,"See brother, didi is not supposed to stay here at all. By staying on here, people like her are creating problems for us."

"So, where should they be?" Rahul wanted to know.

"Why, in India. Bangladesh is a country for Muslims. We don't want anyone but Muslims to live here."

"But there are others who are not Muslims but were born and brought up in this country. Why should they leave their motherland and go away?" Rahul said. By now the two boys had noticed that Rahul spoke Bangla with a different accent.

They asked him, "Are you from Kolkata?"

"Yes, you can say that. But I have come from Delhi."

"You have relatives here?"

"No, I am a journalist."

"Oh, that explains things."

The two boys did not say anything more. They got off at the next stop. Rahul wondered whether the mental torture that the boys had just inflicted on the woman who seemed to be a school teacher, would stand up in the court of law. It would not. Yet this was definitely torture, the sort of behaviour that Hindu women in this country had to put up with at every step.

Rahul met Bibhuti Saha, a schoolteacher from Sonapur, at his house. He said that soon after the caretaker Awami Government handed over the administration to the new Government, his house was bombed. He went and lodged a complaint at the police station which brought on a retaliatory bomb attack. He was beaten up as soon as the government changed and told to take back his report or face dire consequences. He took back his report under coercion. Belal, Kamrul, Didar and others who had beaten him up, had been his students. Bibhuti broke down while narrating this. How could his students do this to him?

Rahul returned from Feni and started his report. "After the change of regime, all the Hindus in Feni have had the same nightmarish experience. In other words they have all been tortured but can't do anything about it. Silently they accepted it as something fated. Weeping parents sent their traumatised daughters to a safer place. Some were ready to go away. Reporting an incident or filing a case could be as the experiences of Bibhuti Saha had shown.

Additional Secretary Nikunja Saha had been killed near the Sahid Minar in Dhaka. The Awami League which was then in power took prompt action so that the killers could be punished and the case did not get caught up in legal formalities and put in cold storage. But the militants made the life of Binod Bihari Nath hell just because he was Nikunja's elder brother. First they demanded large sums of money from him. Then they threatened to kill him. Nothing could be done as the Awami League was no longer in power. There was no one who could help him or give his shelter. He felt absolutely helpless. He desperately wanted some security. Were the Hindus in Bangladesh at all safe, Binod Bihari asked himself. Was it not a shame that a nation could not protect a section of its own people? How would it provide security to other sections of citizens? The Government which had joined hands with extremists had proved that it had lost its credibility. Whenever the right kind of ambience for democracy had been built up in this country, an ambience which could help people in demanding their democratic rights, which disruptive, communal forces had suppressed. And, on all such occasions, Hindus had been victimised. It was the same story right from 1947, when the country had been partitioned. This country had never faced communal riots in that sense because the Hindus had never been able to fight back, they had always been repressed. Many had crossed over in search of security. If they had not left the population of Hindus in this country would have gone up to three crores. But they had gone away on their own, they were forced to.

Eleven

Rahul's visa was about to expire. But he had been told to stay on in Dhaka for a few more days. This morning his editor in Delhi had told him to get his visa extended. Earlier, Bari had helped him to get a visa extension. He wondered whether he should get someone's help or try on his own. After musing for a while, he decided to try himself since he was familiar with the formalities. He proceeded towards the Visa Office. On the way, a little ahead of the Mogbazar Crossing, two men blocked his way, near the Holy Family Hospital. They told the auto driver to stop. Rahul was a little scared wondering if they meant to mug him when they told him to get off. He looked at his watch, it was ten thirty. He told his auto driver to move on, he smiled but did not. Rahul did not have any option but to ask those two who they were. One of them took out his ID card and showed it to Rahul. They were from Special Intelligence and Rahul had to comply. They told him to get into a car parked on the other side of the road.

"Where are we going?" Rahul wanted to know.

"To your hotel."

"Why?'

"You have to pack your bags."

"Why? Where do I have to go?"

"To the airport."

"But why? I still have one day's visa left."

"You have to go back even if you had one month's visa left."

"But why?"

"You are interfering in the internal affairs of this country. Your reports are discrediting Bangladesh to other countries. Anyway, there is no need for us to explain. Come."

Rahul paid off the auto driver and went and sat in the car with the men. After some time the car turned left and stopped at the Shantinagar Crossing after Beli Road. Rahul wanted to make a call before the signal turned green and asked permission. He was told that he could make just one call to his editor in Delhi, no more.

"But I have made friends with so many people here. I want to talk to them before I leave!"

"Talk to them about what?" One of them sounded irritated. He said, "Don't feel insecure. You are safe in our custody. You can tell your editor that. Apart from that you can make no other calls. You don't have the permission."

"Oh, all right." He did not have a choice.

The signal had turned green by now.

As the car stopped at his hotel, the men accompanied Rahul to the reception. One of them took out a slip of paper with the phone number of Rahul's editor on it and gave it to the young man at the counter

Rahul had prepared himself mentally for any eventuality. But he was stunned to see that the man had his editor's mobile number. Before Rahul picked up the receiver, the man who had sounded irritated in the car, told him, "Be brief and speak in Bangla or English, not in Hindi. We don't understand Hindi."

No one had ever spoke to Rahul in that manner. He felt quite humiliated, but controlled himself and took the receiver. He was a little assured when his editor picked up the phone. He told him what had happened and that he was coming back to Delhi. The editor reassured him and said that he himself would come to the airport to receive him.

Rahul told the man at the counter to make his bill and went to his room. The two men from Special Intelligence accompanied him. He packed his bags, told the reception to send someone to carry them down, picked up his handbag and went down to pay his bill and hand over his key. As he went to the car and got in, he noticed that his luggage had already been put in the dickey. The car proceeded towards the airport, passing Shantinagar, Malibag, Mauchak and Rampura. By now Rahul knew that these two men would not harm in any way – their duty was to put him on the plane. He would not be able to go to Agailjhara in Barisal a day later as he had planned. He could have gone there on his way back from Bhola, but that had not been possible as he had been in a hurry. He had wanted to buy some gifts for his wife and daughter, especially a Dhakai Jaindani sari for his wife, maybe some trouser lengths for himself and vests. But that was not to be. Suddenly he realized that they were at the airport. The two men had not spoken a word during the car journey. As he put his bags on the trolley, he told one of the men that his ticket was not even confirmed. He was told that everything would be done. As he went through the immigration counter, he remembered the day he had entered this country two months back. What a difference between the two days! Then he had felt thrilled to come here. And now…

It was a totally different experience. He was not going voluntarily, he was being compelled to go, just because he had sent stories that were based on facts. Was that an offence? Rahul did not believe it was.

He sat in the waiting room. His boarding pass said that his flight was at three forty, it was only two. It was not a straight flight, it would go via Kolkata. The two men were still with him. They were walking around, talking to each other and to the airport staff. Rahul made up his mind not to go Delhi straight but break journey in Kolkata. He would meet his parents in Kolkata and go to Delhi the next day. He would have to wait at the Dhaka airport for another one and a half hours.

Why not take a look at the duty free shops? He stood up and went to the store that said Bangladesh Tourism Corporation. As he looked at the handicrafts inside, he heard the familiar BBC music that played before the news. He listened carefully with the leather item still in his hand. Suddenly he put it down and told the salesman to turn up the volume. It was the voice of the BBC correspondent from Dhaka. He said,"Today Professor

Gopalkrishna Muhuri, Principal, Nazirhat College in Chittagong was attacked and murdered by militants belonging to the Jamat-e-Islam. He was woken up in the morning and shot dead. The Home Minister was in Chittagong when this happened. Jamat-e-Islam is one of the members of the four party alliance. " Rahul could not buy anything after this. He went to a chair outside the store and sat down.

He had visited Prof Muhuri just before the elections and talked to him for quite a while. He had quoted him extensively in the story he had sent that day. Prof. Muhuri had expressed his apprehensions about Hindus going to vote but had not mentioned even once that his life was in danger. Yes, he did say in the course of the long conversation that some of his colleagues who were supporters of Jamat-e-Islam, were eyeing his post. But such things did not worry him. At that time Jamat-e-Islam was not in power, today it was. Rahul asked himself whether it was a pre-planned murder to get the post of the principal for party men.

[illegible] Minoo [illegible] Mr. [illegible] Collins [illegible] were all [illegible] by [illegible] before going to the [illegible] Hotel. He was [illegible] up in the [illegible] and [illegible]. The Heart Murmur [illegible] R [illegible] could not [illegible] anything [illegible] the [illegible] except the store [illegible] down.

At [illegible] the [illegible] he [illegible] for quite a while [illegible] the story he had [illegible] that [illegible] had [illegible] the professional [illegible] but [illegible] mentioned [illegible] in the course of the [illegible] was not [illegible] did not [illegible] planned to [illegible] for [illegible]

there [illegible]

reply [illegible]

loud [illegible]

others [illegible]

was [illegible]

pleasure [illegible]

question [illegible]

Twelve

Rahul came out of the Netaji Subhas Chandra Airport and took Kazi Nazrul Islam Road to go to the city. He planned to go Shyambazar to visit his parents. On the way the taxi driver wanted to know if he was coming from Bangladesh. Rahul just nodded without saying a word. "How is the situation there?" He wanted to know. "Not too good." It was a cryptic reply. As the driver overtook an overcrowded bus, he said in a loud voice, "Would people have come away in such large numbers otherwise?" He did not continue when he noticed that Rahul was not interested. He must have wondered whether his passenger was from Bangladesh or Kolkata, because his next question was," Dada what is your name?"

"Rahul Roy. Why do you ask?"

"Well, I wondered whether you are from Dhaka or Kolkata."

"What do you think?"

"I can't quite make out."

"What is your name?"

"Jadunath Mandal. Once I too lived in Bangladesh – In the Gopalganj sub division of Faridpur."

"Gopalganj is no longer a sub division, it is a full fledged district." Rahul corrected him and asked, "What is the name of the village you came from?"

"Kotalipara."

"I visited it."

"Oh, Dada, really!"

"Yes."

"How many Hindus are still there?"

"I did not count. But there are many. Kotalipara is one of those districts where there are large numbers of Hindus. When did you come?" Rahul wanted to know.

"When General Ershad made Islamic the state religion. Soon after that."

"Oh, is that so!" Rahul said nothing more.

He felt very disturbed today. How could it be otherwise? He would never forget how he had been treated by the Government. But he did not want to discuss this with anyone as yet. Certainly not at present. He had told his editor because he had to. But he would not tell anyone else, certainly not his parents. His father would feel very upset if he told him. He had not reconciled himself to the Partition even now. His eyes brimmed over with tears when anyone talked about Bhola. Talking about today's incidents would only make them feel very sad.

As he pondered over all this, the taxi reached its destination.

He had reached his house, on the crossing of the Badridas Temple Street. He got off and walked down the lane. He noticed his father having tea on the balcony of the second floor of his house. Maybe his mother was downstairs doing the *Sandhya* Puja. As he rang the bell, his father saw him. Rahul forced himself to smile though he did not feel like it, as he looked up at his father. He told the maid to open the door.

He came down even before Rahul could enter the house. His mother had preceded him. Rahul felt like putting his arms round them and crying but controlled himself. He entered the house and told his father, "I did go to Bhola."

"I could make out when I read your story." His father said.

"Sorry, I could not take any photographs of your house."

"So they did not let you take any photographs of the house, did they?"

"No *Baba* that is not what happened. I myself did not take any photographs. But I have got you some earth from there, from a spot near the house."

Saying this, Rahul gave him the handkerchief in which he had tied up some earth. His father put it to his forehead as a mark of respect. His eyes were full of tears. He showed it to Rahul's mother and burst out crying just like a child. Perhaps they would not have been so happy if Rahul had made arrangements for them to go to the moon. The earth was put in a bottle and Rahul's mother was told to keep it in her Puja room so that she could pay her respects to her motherland everyday while doing Puja. Who could be dearer on this earth than one's mother and the motherland was just as dear. It was natural for Rahul's father to feel this way to worship the earth since he could no longer visit the place where he had been born.

After breakfast Rahul called up his editor who told him to stop in Kolkata for a few days Rahul then requested him to arrange for his wife and daughter to come to

Kolkata. The editor did not give him any reason as to why he was supposed to stay on in Kolkata for a few days and said that he would send a fax to the Kolkata

Bureau to that effect. Rahul wanted to spend some time with his parents. After a long time he had got the opportunity to do so. Who knew what the editor would ask him to do the next day! Maybe the editor would assign him some work in Kolkata itself. As he talked to his parents, his eyes fell on the TV screen and he stopped. The newsreader was saying that the people of West Bengal had taken out a procession and demonstrated in front of the Bangladesh Deputy High Commission against the atrocities on Hindus in Bangladesh. The deputy High Commissioner had been given a memorandum. There was a visual of the procession along with the news. After the news, Rahul's father said that a few days back there was news of a young Bangladeshi girl being shot by a BSF soldier in North Dinajpur. She had been trying to cross over as her family had been victimized and was shot at the border. Later the BSF gave the statement that she had been asked to stop but fear had made her run for cover and get killed in the process.

"What do people in West Bengal feel about the large exodus from Bangladesh around the Elections?" Rahul asked his father.

"Some political leaders feels that they are intruders, others are of the opinion that they should be considered refugees and given asylum. The debate is still on. But people are sympathetic towards them, generally speaking, barring some exceptions. When we came away from Bhola it was the same. Some were sympathetic, others were not. The same persons cannot reconcile themselves to this large exodus. Could the new Government in Bangladesh create the right kind of ambience for these people to go back?" Rahul's father wanted to know.

"Impossible!" Rahul's retort was impassioned.

"Why so?"

"Those who have come here will never be welcomed back. The authorities there will never do i. Will you ever consider going back to Bhola? To the place where you were born and brought up?"

"Those were the days of the Partition. Today the situation is different." Rahul's father wanted to calm him. But Rahul would not be pacified. He said, "I don't have first hand experience of how things were during the Partition, my knowledge is based on what you have told me and what I have read in books. But during this visit, what I saw and heard horrified me. I swear that the situation there is as bad as it was in 1947.And, the people who have crossed over recently are in worse shape than you were. You cannot imagine what would happen to these poor people if they are considered intruders and forced to go back by the authorities. They would have just two options before them – continue living there in spite of dishonour, extortion, molestation and rape or face death. Those who cannot do it would keep on coming back to India. Of course they can always go back and convert to the majority religion. That would be the easy way out. What option would you give these poor people who are unwanted in India and oppressed in their own country?" Rahul's father was silent, he had no answer. He had not given the matter such serious thought earlier. Indrabehari Roy felt his heart going out to these poor refugees. It was his duty to something for them. He got up and made a call.

As he put the receiver down Rahul asked him, "Who were you talking to?"

"Ashoka Gupta." Indrabehari said.

"She is part of your group, isn't she? Where will you met tomorrow?"

"At Ashokadidi's place. Some other people are also expected. Shiela Ghosh is one of them."

"Who is she?"

"Gourkishore Ghosh's wife. Tomorrow we are going to discuss how these refugees can be helped. We have to take a decision in this matter. I am going to give fifty thousand rupees from the provident fund money that I got after retirement. Ashokadidi was the person who had made it possible for me to have my own house. If we did not have it, God knows where we might have been today. It was Gourkishore Ghosh who had got me a job. Maybe you know all this."

"Yes father. I know all this. I am proud of the decision that you have taken." Rahul got up and went to his room upstairs.

The next day Rahul heard his daughter's voice when he got up. He was grateful to his editor for sending his wife and daughter to Kolkata by the early morning flight. He had never remained away from his wife for such a long time. He picked his daughter up and looked towards the door at Nandini who was standing there with an envelope in her hand. He beckoned to her.

Nandini was crying as she came to Rahul and hugged him tight. Then she looked up and asked him, "How many days had they detained you?"

"Just a few hours, not days. Who told you all this? Must be the editor."

"Yes" Nandini nodded and handed him the envelope. Rahul got up from the bed. He sent his daughter down and told Nandini everything right from the time he had visited the Holy Family Hospital in Dhaka to the time he was escorted to the airport. He added that he had not talked about to his parents and did not want to.

He read the letter that his editor had sent him, very carefully, at breakfast. The editor had written that he should send daily reports based on interviews with refugees from Bangladesh in West Bengal. The Bureau in Kolkata had been asked to extend all possible help to him in this regard.

Rahul did not know where to find the refugees from Bangladesh in West Bengal. He would have to take help from Suman Bhattacharya, Bureau Chief. He rang him up at home. Suman told him that he had already received instructions from the editor and would make arrangements for him to start work.

"But first I have to do some homework myself." Rahul said.

"What sort of homework?" Suman asked.

"Well the places where these refugees are staying and the extent of help that they are getting from the Government as well as NGOs."

Suman told Rahul that he would brief him on all this when he came to office in the evening.

Thirteen

Hindus who had crossed over from Bangladesh had taken shelter in nine districts of West Bengal. These were located on the Bangladesh West Bengal border. He noted down the names of these districts along with names of those on the border. He wanted to survey these districts and send reports from the next day onwards. The Kolkata Bureau had hired a jeep for his use. Suman suggested that instead of going out of Kolkata he should first meet people working in NGOs and Government agencies as well as organizations backed by political parties as they could tell him about the migrants. Rahul thought it was a good idea and changed his earlier plans.

Rahul met members of the Bangladesh Refugee Welfare Council first. They declared that afte the elections in Bangladesh at least one lakh Hindus had crossed over to India. But the Left Front Government did not quite agree with this figure. According to it the number of Hindus who had crossed over to India was not alarmingly large. It did not mention any figure. However, the Border Security Force, the Central Intelligence Agency and other bodies had been alerted to prevent any large scale crossing over. Despite the Left Front Government not considering it a serious problem, the Union Home Minister Lalkrishna Advani had declared that the situation was serious and needed immediate attention. Subhas Chakravarty, a minister of the Left Front whose views were different from that of his party, also considered the situation serious.

The report of the Commission set up to look into the allegations of atrocities on Hindus in Bangladesh and the fact that they were being forced to leave the country, had been placed before the cabinet. The report stated that no citizen of Bangladesh had left the country after the elections. Only two incidents of atrocities on Hindus were put on record. The Deputy High Commission in Kolkata had said that after investigations, it had been found that there was no truth in the report that Hindus from Bangladesh had taken shelter in any district of West Bengal. There were no Hindus in these places who were citizens of Bangladesh.

On the other hand BJP leader Vijay Kumar Malhotra had demanded that the Hindus who had crossed over from Bangladesh because of oppression should be given refugee status. But the Prime Minister Atal Bihari Vajpeyi had said that India was a secular state and no one forced to flee Bangladesh because of religious reasons should be considered a refugee. The para-military forces at the border had been instructed not to treat any of these Hindus harshly. In spite of these instructions, seventy three persons from different areas of 24 paraganas had been rounded up and put in the Ganarajpur BSF camp. Authorities in this camp were in contact with the Hijaldah BDR camp in the Satkshira district. As the authorities on both sides wasted time writing to each other, the seventy three persons led a miserable life in the refugee camp.

Rahul's eye fell on the three photographs issued by Reuter. Sagarika Ghosh who had come from Badalpur, a village on the India Bangladesh border, four hundred kilometres from Kolkata, had a frightened look on her face as she clutched her son Biswajit to her breast. She had lost all her belongings on the way. Her son was crying with hunger but she had nothing to feed him. She held him tightly to her breast to stop him from crying but the warmth of the mother's breast did not sate his hunger. The other photograph showed Hindu women, some with children in their laps, begging for food in the village of Badalpur. They had never thought that they would be forced to cross the border after the elections and beg for food. In the third photograph, a woman was cooking on a makeshift *chulha* and her three children were waiting behind her with plastic sheets.

Rahul wondered whether to visit Badalpur after he saw those pictures. He was planning to go to Bongaon the next day. He decided to go to Badalpur later, not now. He would visit Bongaon first.

He met more than a hundred families in Bongaon. The frightened Hindu families did not want to go back to the miserable life that they had been leading of late. Most of them were staying here with friends or relatives. They were planning to stay on. They were in hiding as they did not want to be pushed back to Bangladesh by the Indian Government. Naturally they were not ready to reveal their true identity. Rahul met Dipali Adhikari who had crossed over with a family of seven. Her family had gone through a nightmarish experience.Rahul noted down all that Dipali Adhikari told him. Three days after the elections her house was attacked and robbed. A fish pond was the only source of income for the family. The water of this pond was poisoned in their presence. The extortionists demanded a sum of one lakh rupees at knifepoint. Dipali had no option but to agree though she could hardly afford this exorbitant sum. She asked for a week's time. One day before the week was over, she and her family fled under cover of darkness to cross over to India. Hers was not an isolated case. Every Hindu family in her village had to pass through the same ordeal. Women were raped and murdered in villages around hers. As she reached the border, she paid a tout to help them to cross it safely and took refuge in Bongaon.

Rahul met Mitarani Roy in a small village near Thakurnagar railway station. She had just about managed to escape intruders with her baby even as intruders broke into her house and robbed it. On the way she had met some others who were in the same plight. They had travelled through forests and marshy land throughout the night to reach the border and now she had taken refuge here. Since her husband had not been at home that night, he did not know her whereabouts. She did not know whether she would ever meet her husband

Anil Chandra Roy. She did not even know whether he was alive or dead. She broke down and started sobbing, her face hidden by her pallu as she spoke about her son asking for his father every day.

All these visits to places outside Kolkata had tired Rahul out. He was thinking of going back to the city and taking a short rest. But that was not to be. Amnesty International had published a report on the atrocities on Hindus in Bangladesh. He got involved with this report. Earlier a Dhaka based NGO called Aine O Shalis Kendra had filed a writ petition based on a study of three hundred and fifty seven cases. There had been two hearings as well and on both occasions the Government had asked for time. On the second occasion, the Government was given about a month and a half to reply. It was difficult to say when the judgement would be given. Members of the four party alliance, along with local office bearers and officials from different departments of the Government had gone to homes of Hindus who had complained, putting pressure on them to declare publicly that there had been no excesses, no atrocities against them. Before the period granted by the court was over, the Government would try to present affidavits from the complainants in the court so that nothing could be proved against it. It was ironical that whosoever was giving a written statement, said that he or she had not been subjected to any kind of oppression. Only the report of the Amnesty International was absolutely impartial and objective. It said," The Amnesty International is concerned about the grave situation created by large scale atrocities on Hindus. In the eighth General Elections in Bangladesh, the four party alliance emerged victorious under the leadership of the Bangladesh Nationalist Party. Supporters of this alliance attacked Hindus because they suspected that they had voted for the Awami League. Hundreds of Hindus were dispossessed of their ancestral land. Hindu women were raped.

Many Hindus were reportedly murdered." Amnesty International had appealed to the Bangladesh Government to take stock of the situation and punish the guilty. It had also made an eight-point recommendation in this matter.

Rahul felt reassured after reading the report. He was waiting for a report of this nature. It was important that other international human rights organizations like the UNHCHR should also send their reports on this matter.

Rahul had gone to London on a fellowship three years back. There he had met Abdul Gaffar Chaudhury, composer of the song *Amar bhair rakte rangano ekushe February* and had slowly become close to him. Even now they spoke on the phone sometimes. As Rahul sat in the Kolkata Bureau of his newspaper, he suddenly thought of him. Why not ring him up and ask for his views on the current situation in Bangladesh – the recent elections, the four party alliance and the atrocities on Hindus that followed the elections. So he called Chaudhury up and after the usual exchange of pleasantries, he asked him the questions he wanted to. It was as if Gaffar Chaudhury had been waiting for such an opportunity. He started off at once about the new regime – the BNP which had yet to establish itself. It was drunk with power and had lost contact with the masses. From the ivory tower which it had built for itself, it functioned in an arbitrary manner. It had made a list of all those associated with the Awami League along with another one of members of the civil and police personnel who were incorruptible. Justice Shahabuddin Ahmed the President nominee of the Awami League knew about the list. Being the head of the caretaker government, he had given his approval for the list to be given to the army so that the leaders and workers of the Awami League could be arrested, the army did not have the authority to do so. The day orders were passed for the arrest of President Justice Shahabuddin, it was an open secret what the results of the elections would be. The atrocities on Hindus and all those associated with the Awami league that followed, was as inhuman and large scale as the genocide of the Jews by the German police and the Gestapo in the thirties. Shahabuddin did not stop at that. He tried his best to poison the army against the Awami League.

Rahul asked him, "How much truth is there in what you have just told me? Do you have any evidence to prove it?"

Gaffar Chaudhury was aroused now and his voice became more strident, "I have challenged Shahabuddin that if he has any moral courage he should try to prove me wrong. I am going to write about it in the Dhaka newspapers."

"But it was the Awami League which had nominated him President..." Gaffar Chaudhury cut Rahul short and said in a grave voice, "Yes, you are right but take it from me that he had agreed to be the President of the country with Sheikh Hasina at the helm, only after a secret meeting with the BNP and tacit approval from them. Till the army got the green signal, he was hesitant to give his approval. As President during the regime of the caretaker government, he was virtually a puppet in the hands of the army.. Sheikh Hasina respected him as a father figure and he kept up a façade of decency. He used the BNP and the army in such a way that Sheikh Hasina and workers of her party could not imagine in their wildest dreams. This was not only Sheikh Hasina's failing but that of her entire party. In fact the name of

M. A. Sayeed was suggested by Shahabuddin at the behest of the BNP and the army, but still Sheikh Hasina did not suspect anything.

Rahul wanted to know why the army was displeased with the Awami League. Abdul Gaffar Choudhury said that Sheikh Hasina's comments on martial law and military governments in different parts of the world at the UN, was interpreted as a personal criticism by General Pervez Musharraf, the president of Pakistan. The army in Bangladesh had taken it for granted that a government formed by the Awami League would not be in its interest. All this along with Sheikh Hasina's comments about military rule alienated the army and the ISI intensified its activities against the government of Sheikh Hasina. In fact the Pakistani intelligence made a three-point programme to overthrow her government. The three points were, firstly to create panic on a large scale so that people lost confidence in the Awami League Government and considered it incapable of maintaining law and order in the country. Secondly, because of this instability, there was the need for a caretaker government which was not an elected one, at least for five years, so that things could come back to normal. Thirdly, after five years the caretaker government would give permission for general elections, only when the situation would become normal and parliamentary democracy could be reinstated.

This in short was the plan to replace military dictatorship by a civil one. Instead of the parliament the army would be its source of power. Also, instead of the stipulated five years this could continue for an indefinite period. Dr. Kamal Hussain, one of Shahabuddin's advisors, was the brain behind this. The London representative of his Republican Forum had given Gaffar a copy of this plan which had his support as well as blessings though not overtly. He never had the moral courage to support anything openly. By nature he was a spineless person, an opportunist who did not have the power to think independently and take decisions on his own. In these five years he did not do anything apart from what the army briefed him to do. Earlier also, in 1991 when he was the head of the caretaker government, he did not dare to do anything independently. Spineless persons always blame others for their own misdeeds. Now Shahabuddin had Justice Latif-ur-Rehman to work with.

"But what significance did the atrocities on Hindus have in the scheme?" Rahul wanted to know.

It was a well planned campaign. The idea was to marginalize the Hindus in those areas where their number was substantial. The main purpose of this campaign was to finish off the Hindus in Pakistan.

Rahul did not respond to this, he wished Choudhury good night and kept the phone down. Dr Kamal Hussain was the main counsel of the writ filed by the Aine O Shalis Kendra. Was this only an eyewash, he asked himself but could not answer the question. Of course the Kendra had not given him a certified copy of show Cause Notice issued by the court to the government despite repeated requests. But the head of this organization was Sultana Chakraborty, daughter of the poet Sufia kamal. There was still a ray of hope! Rahul did not want to lose faith in humanity.

Fourteen

Rahul visited the Kumarpara-Bhatpara area in 24 Parganas that day. He met Pranab Roy, a journalist who told him that many men and women from Bangladesh who had been tortured, had come to his area through the Darshana Gate border and more were pouring in. Nine members of two families had taken shelter in his house itself. At least fifty refugees crossed over every day with the help of touts. Very few of them had visas or other papers. Those who came with visas had to face many problems. Five days back Ajit Majumdar, his wife and two daughters were crossing over legally. The officials at the Bangladesh border let them cross over but stopped the daughters, both young. They were arrested. When they refused to cross without their daughters, they were forced to. Both of them kept crying for their daughters.

Swapan Kumar Sarkar was one of those who had taken shelter

in Pranab Roy's house. He told Rahul that he had crossed the border as part of a group of three hundred and fifty persons with the help of touts. The tout had charged six hundred taka per person. After crossing over, each person went his or her own way, he did not know about the others. They were grateful to Pranab Roy for giving them shelter. Sarkar would go to Howrah where his aunt lived and look for some work. He had not been able to bring any money and would have to find some way of looking after his family of five. Rahul wondered how Swapan would be able to find work – it was not that easy. Perhaps he would have to spend his life, struggling to make both ends meet in another country, a different ambience. As a teacher in Agailjhara School in Barisal, Swapan Sarkar had perhaps never faced such a difficult situation earlier.

On his way back from Bhatpara, Rahul met Pankaj Banerjee, member of Trinamul Congress and leader of opposition in West Bengal Legislative Assembly. He was coming back after touring the border areas on behalf of his party and taking stock of the situation after having talked to people who had crossed over. Pankaj Banerjee said that the Government should set up refugee camps as he was not in favour of people crossing over and spending their lives in inhuman conditions.

Rahul had to go to Bongaon again, the busiest area on the India-Bangladesh border where most people cross over. Here he met Aghor Saha who told him that five families from the Gaur River region in Barisal had taken shelter in his house. They had left only a day back without really knowing where to go. They had caught a train to Sealdah. There were three families at Gauranga Mandal's house still who were from Bagerhat, Gauranga

Mandal and Aghor were related. When Aghor had gone to see off the five families till Macchhlandpur, he had gone straight to Gauranga Mandal's house from the station.

It was a Sunday and Aghor 's day off, he told Rahul. That was he had stayed on at Gauranga's place when the latter had requested him. He had slept in the outer room at night and could not sleep as the place was new. He had got up on hearing the cry of a child. He had woken Gauranga and the two of them had set out to investigate. Aghor had seen refugees earlier, it was a familiar sight for him but Gauranga was scared and would have retreated if Aghor had no stopped him. They went towards the mango tree near the tap outside and saw a group of ten women and children along with a man. Earlier, the child's cry had woken Aghor up. When they saw Aghor and Gauranga they got scard but felt a little reassured when Aghor introduced himself. Suddenly another child in the group wailed and Aghor was told that it missed its mother.

"Where is the mother?"

"She is not here. Couldn't make it." The man said.

"Why have you brought the child without the mother?"

"Couldn't find the mother." The man said.

"What do you mean, couldn't find her?" Rahul sounded agitated.

When they saw he was agitated, thse who were eating *gur* and *muri* stopped. No one said anything. Suddenly a woman could be heard wailing. Gauranga flashed his torch at him and said that there was no need to feel scared.

The man said that she was not crying out of fear. She was

crying for her sister, perhaps.

"What happened to her?" Aghor had wanted to know.

"She had been kidnapped from her house two days after the elections. Since then she is missing. This is her child."

Aghor could not say anything. Gauranga ran into the house, woke his wife up and brought her along with him. She picked the baby up placed it on her lap, warmed some milk for it. She made *khichdi* for all the others, opened up rooms for them to sleep.

Rahul made Aghor sit in his jeep and turned back to Macchhlandpur. He wanted to talk to the people who had taken shelter in Gauranga Mandal's house.

He met Shefali Sarkar at Gauranga's house and talked to her. Her younger sister had been taken away right under her husband's nose and nothing was known about her even one month later. Her brother-in-law had been admitted to the Sadar Hospital in Bagerhat with serious injuries but even there he was not left alone. He would have been killed if sincere doctors and other employees had not intervened. He had been attacked the second time because he had dared to lodge a report at the police station about his wife.On the same night he was taken out of the Bagerhat Hospital and kept in the house of a relative who lived close to the border. Ultimately, touts were paid a large sum to help him to cross the border. He had been admitted in a clinic in Kolkata where he was being treated for his injuries.

"In which clinic has he been admitted in Kolkata?" Rahul asked.

Sonali said,"I don't know."

"Do you know in which locality the clinic is?"

"No, not even that."

"Will you meet Arun in Kolkata?"

"I do want to meet him."

Rahul did not ask anything else. He had been toid that those who had crossed over in sheer desperation, did not want to reveal their identity as they were afraid of being labelled Bangladeshi and pushed back. On the other hand, the owners of the houses in which they had taken shelter were apprehensive of being arrested for harbouring illegal immigrants. With this reluctance on both sides, it was not possible to find out the numbers of Hindus who had crossed over. The situation was getting more and more complicated. The Hindus who had crossed over and taken shelter in a relative or friend's house would move out to another place, spreading out in villages and small towns of West Bengal. What could they do? There were no refugee camps where they could stay for a short while. None of them were prepared to go back. They wanted to stay on even if it meant hiding their true identities. Rahul asked Sonali Sarkar:

"When will you go back?"

"There is no going back."

"Why?"

"Going back would mean losing both honour and life."

"The Bangladesh Government has said that it will look after your safety and security."

"There is no going back despite what the Government has said. It is not possible. What the Government is saying has nothing to do with the reality. Those who have committed atrocities on us will torture us more if we go back. Earlier they had threatened to kill us and throw our bodies into the river, they will carry out their threat if we go back.

"How can you say this without actualy going back and seeing for yourselves?"

"One does not have to go back to assess the situation."

Rahul did not ask Sonali any more questions. He proceeded towards the Petropole border chowki where he met Shivkumar, a BSF jawan. The latter told Rahul that they knew that Hindus from Bangladesh were crossing over through various forests on the border but they had been ordered not to fire on them. They had been ordered to catch hold of them and push them back into Bangladesh. He said that they had been ordered to behave kindly with them and that is what they were doing.

On their way back, Gauranga Mandal told Rahul that the authorities were not arresting Bangladeshi Hindus on humanitaian grounds. Another thing was that there was always a nexus between the Border Security Force and the touts. Basicaly all political parties agreed that no one shold be forced to go back to Bangladesh, though there was disagreement on their numbers, whether to give them refugee status or not and whether they should be allowed to stay on in India or made to go somewhere else.

Rahul dropped Gauranga Mandal at Bongaon on his way back from Petropole. Then he proceeded towards Kolkata, taking the Jessore Road. Jessore Road! The name itself took one back to an undivided Bengal – the Bengal that Rahul had never seen or experienced. And that was not to be in future as well. As they went down the road in their jeep, they saw fields on both sides, some ploughed and ready to be sown. Rows of date palms with small ponds here and there, farmers tilling the soil, all this reminded Rahul of Bangladesh.There was no difference in landscape. Politicians might have succeeded in dividing the country, but it was beyond them to change the face of nature. Had the political border benefitted anyone, Rahul wondered. It had certainly devastated lives of persons like Sonali Sarkar, the schoolteacher he had met earlier. God knows how many more lives would be lost in future. Rahul remembered what she had told him. She had said, "Right from the beginning we have heard abuses like *malaun* and *malaun baccha*, and put up with it, without retaliating. Even then we have suffered at the hands of those have abused us." Even as he was lost in his thoughts, they had reahed Kolkata, leaving Jessore Road behind, the road that the people of West Bengal had lovingly named after a district in Bangladesh.

In Kolkata Rahul spoke to Biman Bose, one of the leaders of the CPM, the party in power. He told Rahul that it would not be fair to play with the future of the Hindus of Bangladesh. Communal forces should not be used to get political mileage.Those who wanted that relations between India and Bangladesh should remain cordial, had a special responsibility in this matter. They should not allow a political tension to develop on this issue as that could sour the relations between the two countries. For an honourable solution of the problem, the two governments would have to make sincere efforts.

In Dikal, a place in the Maldah district, Rahul met Arun Kumar Roy. He had come from a place called Bidal in Dinajpur. Twenty Hindu families had crossed over with his and all of them had taken shelter in Dikal. Rahul noticed that there was hardly any difference between Bengalis on either side of the border, in dress or features. That is why it was difficult to distinguish them from each other. He recognized Arun Roy at once as he had met him earlier, in Dhaka, at the Dhakeshwari Temple. On 12 October last, the Hindu Buddhist Christian Unity Council had called a meeting in Dhaka where representatives from different areas had described the atrocities on Hindus in their respective areas. Arun had represented his area on that occasion. Rahul had been attracted by his speech and gone and met him. He had wanted to know more about the organization, its activities and plans. Arun had not said anything himself but introduced him to Rana Dasgupta who had told Rahul about the historical background of the Unity Council and its activities. After taking over the Government, General Ershad declared Islam as the national religion and went about his mision of Islamization of the country with a vengeance. Red Cross was renamed Red Crescent and all those who were non-Muslims became second class citizens. Actually the process had started earlier when General Zia-ur-Rehman had deleted the clause that had declared Bangladesh as a secular state in the Constitution. When Islam was declared the naional religion, all others became third class citizens. This Council had been set up by the three significant religious minorities, namely Hindus, Buddhists and Christians to protect their identities. Of course the organization had the support of secular persons from the masjority religion as well. These were the few people who could be called the conscience keepers of the country.

Rahul came back to Kolkata after talking to Arun in Maldah.

He would have liked to talk to a few more refugees but that was not possible. The editor had rung him up and told him to return to Kolkata immediately. He had not given any reasons but told him that he would get to know when he was back.

Rahul passed many ponds and fields but the beauties of nature did not touch him. He remembered Arun again and again. He had taken a bus to his village immediately after the meeting at the Dhakeshwari Temple. After travelling the whole night, he was stopped on way to his house, the house where his family had lived for generations. His great grandfather had written down the names of eleven generations before he passed away. Ainul Haq, the man who stopped Arun, lived nearby and worked for the BNP Alliance in the elections. There were others with him but he was in the forefront. His father, Saijuddin Manjhi had worked for Arun's father and relations between the two families had always been cordial. He had passed away a few years back and Arun had considered it his duty to visit him and condole him. Arun had fond memories of him. He remembered that Saijudin had looked after the horse that his grandfather had, along with his other duties. He remembered one occasion when he had just started going to school. Saijuddin had tied the horse to a *bel* tree and given it grass. Arun was passing that way as usual, watching the colourful birds on the tree. Even to this day he loved looking at birds and it pained him when someone hunted them down. On that day, when he passed the tree, he felt like stroking the horse as he had seen Saijuddin doing. But the horse would have none of it, and shook him off. Arun fell at a little disance and cried out with fear. His screams had brought everyone running. His elder sister picked him up and tried to console him, but he wouldn't stop crying. That day Saijuddin Manjhi had put him on the horse and taken him round the field. He had stopped crying as soon as he had found himself on the horse. After that day the horse had never troubled him and he had never felt scared of it. He had so many fond memoriesd of Saijuddin.

It was his son who had now blocked his way. He had misbehaved with Arun earlier as well, on becoming a member of the Union Council. But Arun had had put up with it, not wanting a confrontation. He was a Hindu, member of a minority community. Ainul was openly contemptuous about Hindus, calling them *Malaun*. Today he could not avoid a confrontation. If he wanted to go to his own house, he would have to talk to Ainul. He wondered what to do, he had nothing to do with Ainul, he did not know what to say to him.

"We have taken possession of this house." Ainul Haq said.

Arun still did not say anything.

"You have to pay us seven lakh taka before you step into it."

Arun was stunned. He felt very helpless. He remembered that Saizuddin Manjhi had brought Ainul along when the latter was to start school, to take the blessings of his master. On that day Ainul had touched Arun's parents feet and then his as well. His father had given Saizuddin a taka along with his blessings. What a difference in the situation then and now!

He kept quiet and sighed.

His wife and child were both at home. As he thought of them he felt more helpless, more worried.

"Your wife and child are both in the school building. You can go and talk to them. But remember that you will have to pay the money I asked for, before you step into your house.

Arun wanted to say many things but thought it would be wiser to keep quiet. Ainul's words had shattered his world. He turned towards the school building to meet his wife and child. Ainul called after him,"Pay up seven lakhs or I keep the house."

Rahul mused over all that he had heard as he went back to Kolkata.

He had met another family in Maldah before talking to Arun Kumar Roy. They had come from Chitalmari in Bagerhat. Generally people who had come to Maldah, Murshidabad and adjoing areas were from the northern part of Bangladesh. Those who had crossed over to Bashirhat, 24 parganas and areas in and around Kolkata were from Barisal , Khulna, Bagerhat, that is to say, the southern part of Bangladesh. As far as Rahul knew this family was an exception. Maybe because the areas near the border were close to each other on all sides, or so he thought.

Prafulla Biswas was the secretary of the local-Union Council. His house was attacked while he gone to office and the marauders started cutting down the plantain trees and supari palms one by one, with a sharp machette.There were only women in the house at that time, and their protests went unheeded. Suddenly the leader of the group lunged towards Sadhana, the college going daughter of Prafulla Biswas. As if this was a signal, the rest attacked the other women present, stripped them and raped them there and then in broad daylight.

Prafulla Biswas broke down, he could not go on. Rahul asked him, "Didn't you report the matter to the police?"

Yes, he had gone to the police station. But the police refused to lodge a report. He was threatened and turned away.

"Did you inform your chairman of the incident?"

"What's the use? The two of them drink together in the evening.I tried meeting the MP but he was not available."

"Was it proper to come away without apprising him of the situation?"

"That would have gien Umer Ali another chance to attack my wife and daughter."

"What are you saying?"

"What I am saying is based on what has happened in Bamgladesh after the elections."

"Maybe it would not happened to you."

"Could the MP stop them from attacking and raping my wife and daughter?"

What could Rahul say? There was no answer to this question. So he kept quiet. He had no more questions for Prafulla Biswas.

Fifteen

President Shahabuddinn Ahmed was one of those who had supervised the Eighth General Elections. It was the Awami League which had nominated him the President of the country. A government official called Ravindranath Trivedi was his Press Secretary. The President treatd him very badly and had no faith in him as he was a Hindu. He had instructed him not to touch his papers. He used to get all his confidential work done by the Assistant press Secretary. Later he banned Ravindranath Trivedi's entry into his office.

The same President who was the Head of the Army, played a dubious role during the Elections, according to General Aslam Haider retd. He said the the entire army along with its officials had been used by him very cleverly against the leaders and supporters of the Awami League.On the polling day the atmosphere was vitiated to the extent that supporters of the

Awami League cold not step out of their homes. The army had acted as an opponent to the Awami League which was not absolutely unfair. Of course a number of persons who were against the Awami League like the President, Chief Secretary and Chief Election Commissioner took special interest in working against the League. It is intriguing why they supported the four party alliance. Their suspicious behaviour and suspicious activities have been taken up by Major Aslam Haider retd, point by point:

a) A seventy year old man was beaten up and held under water. Was he really a terrorist? How can a man who is bent with age, who is not able to move properly, raise his voice against the authorities?

b) A lathi charge would be ordered as soon as a procession of Awami League supporters was seen . On the other hand, a similar procession of BNP supporters would be allowed to proceed or ignored.

c) Supporters of the Awami League were terrorised in many ways. Tying a rope round their waists and parading them in public like common criminals shamed them and deterred other supporters from casting their votes.

d) Homes of the Awami League supporters were searched. This was done intentionally to harrass them so that they were compelled to leave their homes or else stop campaigning for the League.

e) The polling agents and party workers of the League were harrassed to the extent that they felt discouraged and did not challenge the illegal activities of their opponents.

f) On the polling day itself, arrangements were made in such a way that the opponents could capture a booth easily if they thought it woyld benefit their party. To achieve this, supporters of the Awami League were beaten up and driven away from those booths.

g) The candidates of the Awami League were constantly insulted and ignored. Candidates from the alliance were helped in many ways so as to make it clear that they had a feeling of hostility towards their opponents.

h) The booths which the supporters of the four party alliance felt would go against them, were specially targeted for creating an atmosphere of terror so that supporters of the Awami League would be scared to come near them, let alone vote. Members of the alliance and their supporters were free to do what they wanted. On the other hand nothing was done to safeguard the booths which the Awami League had indicated wold go against them. So the four party alliance managed to manipulate the situation and won the so called 'impartial' elections.

The main thrust of Major Haider's critical comments is that the President could not shake off his accountability, being the Head of the armed forces. It could not be believed that all thiese incidents took place without his knowledge.The four party alliance which was made after the elections,was a suppoter of Taliban. In fact one of the parties of the alliance coined the slogan 'All of us are Talibal/Bangladesh will become Afghan'. Apart from that the two persons from a different party who had been made ministers by the Alliance Government, were both supporters of Taliban. As soon as the Taliban came into power in Afghanistan, they had been supporting the Taliban-Jamate Islam Government there. This party has shown an active interest in promoting pro-Talibal ideals. Pictures of Osama bin Laden were put up, not only in Dhaka but in other parts of the country as well, in public places, offices and shops. The alliance government never stopped such activities but encourages them. Even common people had now started hanging Osma's picture in their homes.

The three parties which had joined up with the BNP to form the four party alliance are, Jamate Islam, a group that had split from the National Party and the Islamic Unity Group. Jamate Islam and Islamic Unity Group had openly criticised the freedom fighters for splitting Pakistan, at a public meeting held in Manik Miah Avenue in Dhaka. On 26 April 1999 there was a congregation of Maulavis in Gopalganj. It was announced at this congregation that the Taliban Government would soon be set up. Even the time for the Taliban Revolution was announced. People like Fazlul Haq Amins, Shaikhul Hadis, Azizul Haq and many others were present on this occasion. Most of them are associated with the Aliance today.

The main speaker Hafiz Umer was made to contest the Gopalganj seat against Sheikh Hasina. In the Narail constituency, another one from which she contested the elections, another candidate who had supported Taliban vociferously, was put up against her. In his election , he had openly declared that he was very close to Osama bin Laden and had gone to Afghanistan for training in Taliban idealism and strategies.

Thus Taliban entered the political scene in Bangladesh openly, defiantly.Those who declared at the Parade Ground in Dhaka that Bangladesh would be ruled by Taliban, were now part of the Four Party Alliance and very close to the Prime Minister of the country. If the government ever became absolutely fundamentalist, Prime Ministe Khaleda Zia would be made to wear a black burqa and confined to her home in the name of Islam as the Taliban had done with women in Afghanistan. Though the fundamentalists had agreed to her leadership on this occasion, it did not follow that thy would do so in future as well.They were only using her to make their own positions secure and would accept her as leader only so long as they cold use her. Sooner or later they would show their true colours, which they have started. With their support Khaleda Zia had managed o secure just forty six percent votes whereas Sheikh Hasina managed to get forty one per cent votes on her own. The Hindu votes accounted for about twelve per cent of the total and this time none of them had been allowed to exercise their franchise as they were considered the vote bank of the Awami League. If the Hindus had not been prevented from voting through rigging snd other methods of election rigging, the results would have been quite different from what they were now. For instance in one polling centre of Patuakhali hundred per cent votes were cast for Mirzaganj Parliamentary seat. But the Awami League did not get a single one whereas, earlier in the General Elections held in 1992, the Awami League had won this seat by 364 votes. This time, not a single Hindu was allowed to vote along with supporters of the Awami League.

Not only were Hindus stopped from casting their votes throughout the country, those who managed to vote were subjected to torture. This is not to say that those who had not voted were spared. Even small children were killed as the fundamentalists felt that they would grow up to support the

Awami League. It was indeed a crime to be born into a Hindu family!

The BBC telecast a report of the atrocities on Hindus with photographs to substantiate it. The AFP had sent in the report afte thorough investigation. Amnesty International had brought out a list of the murders and rapes. Even then the Government was trying to black out what had happened. Why were they doing this? Their evasive attitude clearly indicated that they had a hand in whatever had happened. There were some intelectuals on the pay roll of the four Party Alliance who came forward to say that much was being made of communalism in the country. If a few sporadic incidents *had* occurred, why should such a fuss be made bout them? They said that it was a good thing that members of the minority community were crossing over to India, where they would be able to merge with the majority community. A government which supported such discrimination and aggression was likely to turn a blind eye to oppression of minorities. It ws more than likely that in such a set up, aggressors were most likely to find shelter as had happened in Bangladesh. If the Government did not punish those who broke the laws of the country, it would be considered guilty by implication. It was difficult to believe that the Four Party Alloance was not aware of this. If it were aware and still feigned ignorance, that was a greater crime. A social set up which did not protest against what it considered wrong, would be implicitly party to it a blame that the intelligentsia would have to shoulder to a large extent. Were the intellectuals, who had sold their souls to the Four Party Alliance, did not know this? If not, they surely knew about the Bengali intellectual called Hassan Firdausi whose conscience troubled him to the extent that he had remarked, "Alas! I wish that the troubles faced by our sisters in villages gave you the moral courage to speak out against what they were facing."

He said, "Even a month ago I did not know that there was a village called Chor Annada Prasad in the Bhola district. Now I know, not only the name of the village but also that of many of those who live there. I have seen their pictures as well. Pictures of girls who look scared to death! Girls whose eyes reflect the shame and pain of the honour that they have lost. I have seen pictures of two girls who have covered their faces with cloth. Only two eyes were visible-eyes that viewed the world helplessly. I try to look for hatred in those eyes but vannot find it. Only fear! A girl peeps from behind a wall. I can see only her eyes, brimming over with tears. I can see the picture of an old woman and a middle aged one, who have lost their honour and their home. Now they have nowhere to go, no shelter except this patch of green under the sky."

If you are not moved by this conscience raiser from Hassan Firdausi, nothing will move you, not even the words of well established intellectuals.If that is the case it is difficult to believe that you have any trace of humanity left. What then can one call such heartless, terrible creatures? They do not deserve to be called human beings.

The number of Hindus in Bangladesh has dwindled with continuing communal aggression. Now it is only seven pe cent of the population. This is because many people believe that it can never be a country where Hindus can stay as well. Most Muslims strongly felt that this was not their country though they might have born here and lived here all their lives. That was the most dreadful thing for the Hindus here. The Hindus here had no life left. Their women could not go out of their homes. Most of them were living on borrowed days, a little like Willie Chandran, the hero of Naipaul's novel *Half A Life.* The Hindus here did not say 'namaskar' or 'adab' when they meet for the first time, they said '*Assalamu Aleikum.*' They had been forced into this and now it has become a habit. This is a survival tactic. Naipaul could easily travel to Bangladesh and write another novel on what was happening here. If the extermination of Hindus goes on, a time will come when there will be no Hindus left in this country.The country which had 33.1 per cent of Hindus, in 1901, had only 7 per cent left today. This meant that 26 per cent of them had been driven away If this could take place in just one hundred years, it would not take them long to drive away the remaining 7 per cent.

Sixteen

Rahul talked to his editor after coming back from his tour of districts of West Bengal. The editor gave him the address of a website and told him to visit it before sending his story. In fact he had told him to return to Kolkata as he could not have accessed it from Maldah. Rahul did not find anything new when he visited the specified website. Rahul had seen whateve there was, in the course of his visit to Bangladesh. This website called 'Drishtipat' had been started by an organization of Bengalis in the US. Rahul came to know about another organization called 'Cheye Dekho' which had tried to project the atrocities on Hindus in Bangladesh to the rest of the world in order to make people aware of the extent of oppression so that something could be done to stop it. But Rahul did not really know whether these things mattered. It was fine to tell the world about the oppression of Hindus, but it was equally important for the

Hindus of Bangladesh to unite and take a stand against against it. However, in a situation where the state supported the oppression in a well planned methodical manner, one could not think of protesting. Rahul could find no solution to the problem. The only ray of hope in an overall bleak situation was that a few persons did, from time to time, act as the conscience of the nation. But the number of those persons was dwindling day by day.

Rahul left his home on receiving a call from Suman. He reached the Ballyganj Station. If one walked a little ahead towards the right, there were slums on both sides. The number of people in these slums went up every day. None of the people who lived here had been born in West Bengal, they had all come from Bangladesh. The Hindus who had crossed over after the elections, had started living here, with people whom they knew or in the homes of their relaties. But none of them were willing to reveal his or her identity because they were scaed that the police might push them back if they did so.Suman had learnt about them from his sources and had passed the information to Rahul.Rahul took a member of the CPI(M) with him and visited many of the slums. It was not possible to visit the whole of it in one day, but he managed to meet quite a few persons.They agreed to talk to him provided he did not ask them to reveal their identity.

The first person he met was Jogesh Chandra Das, a doctor from Jhinaidah, Bangladesh. He said that neither he nor his family had not been attacked but he had been an eye witness to atrocities on many persons. They were threatened that if there was trouble in Babri Mosque or a war between India and Pakistan, they would be finished off. They had received this threat ealier but when they saw what was happening all round them after the elections, the full implication of it dawned on them. Jogesh Chandra told Rahul that the militants had been slightly intimidated by teams of observers and journalists, but they continued with their threats. After all journalists and NGOs could not always come to their help. Some people had been so scared that they stopped sending their children to school. A student of class nine did not go to school for a single day after the elections.Savita, daughter of Manoranjan Das, a student of class five, was also in the same boat. Her parents had sent her here with Jogesh Chandra Das. But she was not here. A relative from her mother's side had taken her to Bardhaman to his home.

Rahul went to Banmali Bhaumik after talking to Jogesh Chandra Das. Banamali was from Bhola district and a supporter of the Awami League. On the day following the elections, his sister-in-law was raped. He himself managed to flee from with his wife and child and go into hiding on the day of election. His neighbour Chiru Das' wife was raped in front of her two children the same day. An old uncle of Chiru Das was sitting near the railway tracks. When Rahul went to him, he gave vent to his feelings, "Our mothers, wives and sisters have been raped publicly. Those who recognize them and point them out to others, are the first to rape them.Since we cannot live honourably there, we have come to a place where no one knows us. Shefali, a neighbour of Bijon Das, had sent her daughter to this place so that she was safe from fundamentalists. She and her husband were still there, hoping to sell off their land before crossing over.The price of land had come down by 25 per cent, still there were no buyers,

Bijon Das said. Some times one did not even know whether one would get the money in hand after selling land. Bijon Das also told him that many Hindus were implicated in false cases or threatened that they would be, if they did not leave or pay up. Some paid up as they did not want to get implicated falselyIn Lalmohan village in Bhola, the leader of a political party that was part of the Alliance, filed cases against sixty five persons and withdrew them only when they paid up five thousand rupees each. Even after paying up, they were threatened that if they revealed the names of those to whom they had paid the money, they would be driven out of the country.

Bijon Das had not yet completed what he had to say. He told Rahul, "We used to live in the Harding Union, a place which had a Hindu majority earlier. The Chairman and members were selected from among us. This was the situation before 1992.At that time Dashrath Babu used to be our Chairman. But after the Babri Mosque incident we faced such oppression that our numbers dwindled to one third of what it used to be. Hindus have always been victims of communal violence and after killing them or driving them away, Muslims have forcibly occupied their land. After '92 we never had a Hindu Chairman."

Rahul walked on, leaving a few slums behind. He met Dulal Karmakar from a village called Chartofazzal in Bagerhat. He had a daughter called Aparna. Though poor, Dulal had many aspirations about his daughter, who grew up, like others of her age, looking at the world with eyes filled with wonder. On the night of 13 October, all Dulal's dreams were shattered as her daughter fell a prey to the lust of the so called nationalists and he could just watch on helplessly. He did not seem mentally stable to Rahul. He stopped in the middle of what he was saying and refused to go on. His wife told Rahul not to ask him any more questions. Rahul lit a cigarette and offered another to Dulal. As Dulal started smoking it, he broke down and started sobbing. He remembered that the fundamentalists had burnt Aparna's private parts with a cigarette and threw it away.

Rahul asked, "Where is Aparna now?"

"Out there." He said, pointing towards to the sky.

Rahul asked, "Did she die on 13 October itself?"

"No. After that inhuman assault, my daughter fell ill and was admitted to the Charfashion Hospital.But the doctor said that she would have to be taken to Dhaka. I brought her home and made preparations to go to Dhaka the next day."

"Did she die on the way?" Rahul wanted to know.

"No, she left us the same night."

What had happened was that Aparna was sitting in the outer courtyard of her home. The Imam of the village mosque was passing that way with his assistant. As his eyes fell on her, he exclaimed,"Oh you slut!" and lowered his umbrella so as not to see her as that would make him impure. After all he had just done his *wazu.* Ironically his elder son Abu Baker was among those who had raped Aparna. The fifteen year old girl had fainted when the rapists had tortured her and burned her with cigarettes. But the Imam's words hurt her even more and she dragged her badly injured body into the house with the help of the stick without which she could not move.Her mother had gone to the pond for her bath and her father had gone to make arrangements for going to Dhaka the next day.

There was no one in the house. She bolted the door from inside and hanged herself so that she did not have to hear such words again.

She was cremated that very night to avoid harrassmnent from the police. But the police did get to know and reached the spot even as the flames were devouring Aparna's body. Her father was handcuffed and arrested as he had not got an autopsy of his daughter's body done and kept in the lock up for three days. There was an out of court settlement between Abu Baker and Dulal under police supervision. Whatever Dulal had saved was handed over to Abu Baker by his wife and he was made to sign on stamp paper before he could be released. As he was released, Abu Baker told him that he had signed away his house, land and the shop in the market to him and had no right to them any more. Where could he go now? He and his wife started on their journey, not really knowing where to go. After wandering a lot, they had come to this place by the railway lines.

Rahul wrote a long story on the basis of his conversations with the people he had met near the Majhirhat railway lines and sent it to his editor. He wrote, "There is no race known as the Muslims, many persons from different communities have converted to Islam. Similarly there is no race known as the Hindus. These are just two different religions. But the Hindus of Bangladesh are Bengalis and they are being wiped out in an attempt to establish a sort of Bengali nationalism. General Zia ur Rahman was the person who started this when he captured the highest power by force, at gunpoint. But it is not possible to set up a communal Bangladeshi nation. That is why it was considered necessary to eliminate the Hindus. The Bangladeshi nation would be based on their graves as it had happened in Pakistan. But Hindus are the products of this country, they were born here, they are ethnically the original residents of this country. Then?

Tranlator's Note

Translation is possibly the most intimate kind of reading that a book can be subjected to. When I started reading *Shameless,* I was so appalled that I actually felt sick. Years ago, another book had affected me the same way. That was about the genocide of Jews in pre-World War II Germany, a book called *Judgement at Nuremburg.*I felt that this book that is *Shameless*, should be translated into as many languages as possible so that people come to know about what is happening in Bangladesh. That is how I started translating it, a page or two at a time because after that I would feel too overcome to go on.

While I was translating the book I met Salam Azad the author, from Bangladesh. He told me that nothing in the book was fabricated or even exaggerated. He had visited the affected areas after the elections and experienced for himself what the protagonist Rahul is supposed to have seen. After seeing the carnage, he fell ill and had to be hositalized. He said that he was so sick that he could not eat or drink anything and could not stop retching. After a few days in the hospital, he realized that he had to get it out of his system and started writing about what he had seen. This had a cathartic effect on him and made him feel better. That was how the book came to be written. He wanted it to be translated into as many languages as possible and I could see his point.

It is difficult to take the book out of its ethnic context, equally difficult to render some of it into English. In some cases, I have not translated words but let them be, italicizing them so that the English language reader, not from the Indian sub-continent, can find out more about them, if interested.It was difficult to translate some of the emotional content into English which is by and large, a staid and prosaic language, but I have made an effort.Of course there would be scope for improvement, no translation is perfect.I hope that I have been able to convey the agony of a people uprooted from their ancestral land, subjected to physical torture and rape, forced to flee to another country for their own safety and the safety of their loved ones.In today's world, the so-called ethnic cleansing has led to a lot of bloodshed and horror. With growing public awareness of them, one can hope that they do not recur as evil needs cover and does not dare to operate in the open. Religious fundamentalism is growing in the world today. Unless checked, it will turn into an uncontrollable monster like Frankestein. That is where the worth of a book like this lies. That is why I have not tried to shorten any passage that evokes horror as that is the purpose of the book. I hope that this book is read by many, who are moved by it to the exent that they protest atively. Only a concerted worldwide effort will check such carnage.